LEVEL AR POINTS
4.9      4

W9-BPN-768

SC      Saldana, Rene
Sal     Finding our way

DISCARD

DEMCO

3400/796

# FINDING OUR WAY

Also by René Saldaña, Jr.
*The Jumping Tree*

✦ STORIES ✦

# FINDING OUR WAY

## René Saldaña, Jr.

WENDY
LAMB
BOOKS

INSTRUCTIONAL MEDIA CENTER
GRISSOM MIDDLE SCHOOL
MISHAWAKA, INDIANA

Published by
Wendy Lamb Books
an imprint of
Random House Children's Books
a division of Random House, Inc.
New York

Copyright © 2003 by René Saldaña, Jr.

All rights reserved. No part of this book may be reproduced or transmitted in any form
or by any means, electronic or mechanical, including photocopying, recording, or by
any information storage and retrieval system, without the written permission of the
publisher, except where permitted by law. Earlier versions of two stories appeared
previously: "Finding Our Way" © 2000 *Georgia State University Review.*
"SylvieSylvieSylvie" © 2002 *Black Mountain Review* (Ireland).

Wendy Lamb Books is a trademark of Random House, Inc.

Visit us on the Web! www.randomhouse.com/teens
Educators and librarians, for a variety of teaching tools, visit us at
www.randomhouse.com/teachers

Library of Congress Cataloging-in-Publication Data

Saldaña, René.
    Finding our way / René Saldaña, Jr.
        p. cm.
    Contents: The good Samaritan—Chuy's beginnings—SylvieSylvieSylvie—Los
Twelve Days of Christmas—Andy and Ruthie—Arturo's troubles—Ain't nothing nor
nobody—My self myself—Un faite—Manny calls—The dive—Finding our way.
    ISBN 0-385-73051-9—ISBN 0-385-90077-5 (lib. bdg.)
    1. Mexican Americans—Juvenile fiction. 2. Children's stories, American.
[1. Mexican Americans—Fiction. 2. Short stories.]    I. Title.
PZ7.S149Fi 2003
[Fic]—dc21
                                                                                    2002008249

The text of this book is set in 13-point Chaparral.
Book design by Melissa J Knight

Printed in the United States of America

March 2003
10  9  8  7  6  5  4  3  2  1
BVG

*✦ ✦ ✦*

*För Kristina Ann Saldaña,
mitt hjärtas flamma,
kvinnan i mitt liv*

*y*

*para mi abuelo
Federico Garcia,
the greatest storyteller*

# ACKNOWLEDGMENTS

Once again, I thank God for this book, and my parents, René, Sr., and Ovidia.

I also would like to thank the following for their support in various ways: Kelly Delong, John Holman, David Rice, Edwardo Saldaña, the many authors whose work I read in the past two years who, unbeknownst to them, acted as my teachers (I hope I've proven myself a good student), Sue Tierney, all at 2843, and countless others.

# CONTENTS

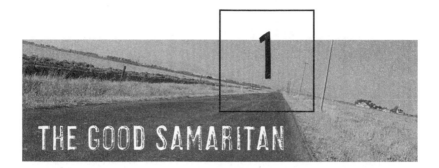

# THE GOOD SAMARITAN

I know he's in there, I thought. I saw the curtains of his bedroom move, only a little, yes, but they moved.

Yesterday Orlie told me, "Come over tomorrow afternoon. We'll hang out by the pool."

I rang the doorbell again. Then I knocked.

The door creaked open. The afternoon light crept into the dark living room inch by slow inch. Mrs. Sánchez, Orlie's mom, stuck her head through the narrow opening, her body hidden behind the door. "Hi, Rey, how can I help you?"

"Ah, Mrs. Sánchez, is Orlando here?" I tried looking past her but only saw a few pictures hanging on the wall. One of the Sánchez family all dressed up fancy and smiling, standing in front of a gray marble background.

"No, he's not. He went with his father to Mission."

"Oh, because Orlando said he would be here, and told me to come over."

"They won't be back until later tonight," she said. "You can come by tomorrow and see if he's here. You know how it is in the summer. He and his dad are always doing work here and there. Come back tomorrow, but call first."

"It's just that he said I could come by and swim in your pool. Dijo, 'Tomorrow, come over. I'll be here. We'll go swimming.'"

"I'm sorry he told you that, but without him or my husband here, you won't be able to use the pool," me dijo Mrs. Sánchez.

"Okay," I said.

"Maybe tomorrow?"

"Yeah, maybe."

But there was no maybe about it. I wouldn't be coming back. Because I knew that Orlando was in the house, he just didn't want to hang out. Bien codo con su pool. Plain stingy. And tricky. This guy invited me and a few others over all summer to help his dad with some yard work because Mr. Sánchez told us, "If you help clean up the yard, you boys can use the pool any time you want so long as one of us is here." And we cleaned up his yard. On that hot day the water that smelled of chlorine looked delicious to me. And after a hard day's work cleaning his yard, I so looked forward to taking a dip. I'd even worn my trunks under my work clothes. Then Mr. Sánchez said, "Come by tomorrow. I don't want you fellas to track all this dirt into the pool."

—"We can go home and shower and be back," said Hernando.

"No, mejor que regresen mañana. I'll be here tomorrow and we can swim. After lunch, okay. For sure we'll do it tomorrow," said Mr. Sánchez.

The following day he was there, but he was headed out right after lunch and he didn't feel safe leaving us behind without supervision. "If one of you drowns, your parents will be angry at me and..." He didn't say it, but he didn't need to. One of our parents could sue him. And he needed that like I needed another F in my Geometry I class! Or, we figured out later, he could have just said, "I used you saps to do my dirty work. And I lied about the pool, suckers!"

I don't know why we hadn't learned our lesson. Twice before he had gypped us this way of our time and effort. Always dangling the carrot in front of our eyes, then snatching it away last second.

One of those times he promised us soft drinks and snacks if we helped clean up a yard across the street from his house. It wasn't his yard to worry about, but I guess he just didn't like to see the weeds growing as tall as dogs. What if he had company? What would they think? And he was angling for a position on the school board. How could a politico live in such filth!

Well, we did get a soft drink and chips, only it was one two liter bottle of Coke and one bag of chips for close to ten of us. We had no cups, and the older, stronger boys got dibs on most of the eats. "I didn't know there'd be so many of you," he said. "Well, share. And thanks. You all are good, strong boys."

The next time was real hard labor. He said, "Help me dig these holes here, then we can put up some basketball rims. Once the cement dries on the court itself, you all can come over and play anytime since it's kind of your court too. That is, if you help me dig the holes."

And we did. We dug and dug and dug for close to six hours straight until we got done, passing on the shovel from one of us to the next. But we got it done. We had our court. Mr. Sánchez kept his word. He reminded us we could come over to play anytime, and we took special care not to dunk and grab hold of the rim. Even the shortest kid could practically dunk it because the baskets were so low. But we'd seen the rims all bent down at the different yards at school. And we didn't want that for *our* court.

One day, we wanted to play a little three on three. After knocking on the different doors several times and getting no answer, we figured the Sánchez family had gone out. We decided that it'd be okay to play. We weren't going to do anything wrong. The court was far enough from the house that we couldn't possibly break a window. And Mr. Sánchez had said we could come over any time we wanted. It was *our* court, after all. Those were his words exactly.

A little later in the afternoon, Mr. Sánchez drove up in his truck, honking and honking at us. "Here they come. Maybe Orlando and Marty can play with us," someone said.

Pues, it was not to be. The truck had just come to a standstill when Mr. Sánchez shot out of the driver's side. He ran up to us, waving his hands in the air like a crazy man, first saying, then screaming, "What are you guys doing here? You all can't be here when I'm not here."

"But you told us we could come over anytime. And we knocked and knocked, and we were being very careful."

"It doesn't matter. You all shouldn't be here when I'm not home. What if you had broken something?" he said.

"But we didn't," I said.

"But if you had, then who would have been responsible for paying to replace it? I'm sure every one of you would have denied breaking anything."

"Este vato!" said Hernando.

"Vato? Is that what you called me? I'm no street punk, no hoodlum. I'll have you know, I've worked my whole life, and I won't be called a vato. It's Mr. Sánchez. Got that? And you boys know what—from now on, you are not allowed to come here whether I'm home or not! You all messed it up for yourselves. You've shown me so much disrespect today you don't deserve to play on my court. It was a privilege and not a right, and you messed it up. Now leave!"

Hernando, who was fuming, said, "Orale, guys, let's go." He took the ball from one of the smaller boys and began to run toward the nearest basket. He slowed down the closer he came to the basket and leapt in the air. I'd never seen him jump with such grace. He floated from the foul line, his long hair like wings, all the way to the basket. He grabbed the ball in both his hands and let go of it at the last moment. Instead of dunking the ball, he let it shoot up to the sky; then he wrapped his fingers around the rim and pulled down as hard as he could, hanging on for a few seconds. Then the rest of us walked after him, dejected. He hadn't bent the rim even a millimeter. Eventually Orlie talked us into going back when his dad wasn't home. His baby brother, Marty, was small and slow, and Orlie wanted some competition on the court.

Today was it for me, though. I made up my mind never to go back to the Sánchezes'. I walked to the little store for a Fanta Orange. That and a grape Popsicle would cool me down. I sat on the bench outside, finished off the drink, returned the bottle for my nickel refund, and headed for home.

As soon as I walked through our front door, my mother said, "Mi'jo, you need to go pick up your brother at summer school. He missed the bus."

"Again? He probably missed it on purpose, 'Amá. He's always walking over to Leo's Grocery to talk to his little girlfriends, then he calls when he needs a ride." I turned toward the bedroom.

"Come back here," she said. So I turned and took a seat at the table. "Have you forgotten the times we had to go pick you up? Your brother always went with us, no matter what time it was."

"Yeah, but I was doing school stuff. Football, band. He's in summer school just piddling his time away!"

She looked at me as she brushed sweat away from her face with the back of her hand and said, "Just go pick him up, and hurry home. On the way back, stop at Circle Seven and buy some tortillas. There's money on the table."

I shook my head in disgust. Here I was, already a senior, having to be my baby brother's chauffeur.

I'd driven halfway to Leo's Grocery when I saw Mr. Sánchez's truck up ahead by the side of the road. I could just make him out sitting under the shade of his truck. Every time he heard a car coming his way, he'd raise his head slightly, try to catch the driver's attention by staring at him, then he'd hang his head again when the car didn't stop.

I slowed down as I approached. Could he tell it was me driving? When he looked up at my car, I could swear he almost smiled, thinking he had been saved. He had been leaning his head between his bent knees, and I could tell he was tired; his white shirt stuck to him because of all the sweat. His sock on one leg was bunched up at his ankle like a carnation. He had the whitest legs I'd ever seen on a Mexican. Whiter than even my dad's. I kept on looking straight; that is, I made like I was looking ahead, not a care in the world, but out of the corner of my eye I saw that he had a flat tire, that he had gotten two of the lug nuts off but hadn't gotten to the others, that the crowbar lay half on his other foot and half on the ground beside him, that his hair was matted by sweat to his forehead.

I knew that look. I'd probably looked just like that digging those holes for *our* basketball court, cleaning up his yard and the one across the street from his house. I wondered if he could use a cold two-liter Coke right about now! If he was dreaming of taking a dip in his pool!

I drove on. No way was I going to help him out again! Let him do his own dirty work for once. He could stay out there and melt in this heat for all I cared. And besides, someone else will stop, I thought. Someone who doesn't know him like I do.

And I knew that when Mr. Sánchez got home, he'd stop at my house on his walk around the barrio. My dad would be watering the plants, his evening ritual to relax from a hard day at work, and Mr. Sánchez would mention in passing that I had probably not seen him by the side of the road so I hadn't stopped to help him out; "Kids today," he would say to my dad, "not a care in the world, their heads up in the clouds somewhere." My dad would call me out and ask me to tell him and Mr. Sánchez why I hadn't helped out a neighbor when he needed it most. I'd say, to both of them, "That was you? I thought you and Orlie were in Mission taking care of some business, so it never occurred to me to stop to help a neighbor. Geez, I'm so sorry." Or I could say, "You know, I was in such a hurry to pick up my brother in La Joya that I didn't even notice you by the side of the road."

I'd be off the hook. Anyways, why should I be the one to extend a helping hand when he's done every one of us in the barrio wrong in one way or another! He deserves to sweat a little. A taste of his own bad medicine. Maybe he'll learn a lesson.

But I remembered the look in his eyes as I drove past him. That same tired look my father had when he'd get home from work and he didn't have the strength to take off his boots. My father always looked like he'd been working for centuries without any rest. He'd sit there in front of the television on his favorite green vinyl sofa chair and stare at whatever was on TV. He'd sit there for an hour before he could move, before he could eat his supper and take his shower, that same look on his face Mr. Sánchez had just now.

What if this were my dad stranded on the side of the road? I'd want someone to stop for him.

"My one good deed for today," I told myself. "And I'm doing it for my dad really, not for Mr. Sánchez."

I made a U-turn, drove back to where he was still sitting, turned around again, and pulled up behind him.

"I thought that was you, Rey," he said. He wiped at his forehead with his shirtsleeve. "And when you drove past, I thought you hadn't seen me. Thank goodness you stopped. I've been here for close to forty-five minutes and nobody's stopped to help. Thank goodness you did. I just can't get the tire off."

Thank my father, I thought. If it weren't for my father, you'd still be out here.

I had that tire changed in no time. All the while Mr. Sánchez stood behind me and a bit to my left saying, "Yes, thank God you came by. Boy, it's hot out here. You're a good boy, Rey. You'll make a good man. How about some help there?"

"No, I've got it," I answered. "I'm almost done."

"Oyes, Rey, what if you come over tomorrow night to my house? I'm having a little barbecue for some important people here in town. You should come over. We're even going to do some swimming. What do you say?"

I tightened the last of the nuts, replaced the jack, the flat tire, and the crowbar in the bed of his truck, looked at him, and said, "Thanks. But I'll be playing football with the vatos."

# CHUY'S BEGINNINGS

Mr. Gutierrez told me, "Come with me, Chuy." On the way to the office he was walking fast in front of me, making like I wasn't even there, and I could've just turned down a ramp and took off running to Leo's Grocery, played hooky the rest of the day, played on the Centipede video game. He wouldn't've ever noticed me gone. Like I was invisible.

He just kept walking while I kept asking, "What's the matter, Mr. G?" No answer, so I said, "Vato, you think you're God?"

"In *my* classroom, I *am* God!" Mr. Gutierrez screamed at me just outside the principal's office. He'd been walking so fast that when he turned around, he caught me off guard and I almost ran into him.

Ah, you ain't nothing, I thought.

A few minutes back, he'd kicked me out of his class for just talking. "Step outside and wait to the right of the door, and don't move from there, Chuy," he'd said.

"Orale," I said.

When he came out, he didn't even explain why he'd yelled at me, just stood there and looked at his watch, his back to me the whole time, until one of the office aides showed up and he said to her, "They know what they're supposed to be doing. I'll try not to take too long."

So now outside the office I told him, "Whatever, God." I took hold of the doorknob, swung open the door, and said, "Well, let's do this thing."

"Let's," he said.

Sure enough, when we got in to see Mrs. Mendez, Gutierrez told her his side of the story: "I've warned Chuy several times already," he began. "And I've got the paperwork to prove it."

Mrs. Mendez listened, her scalp showing through her thinning hair, shining in the light coming through the window behind her. When she raised a finger to speak, he kept on going, he waved her off: "And believe you me, Mrs. Mendez, I've put enough energy into this Time Out strategy this school district has adopted, especially with Chuy, too much energy and time, time I could be spending with the students who are in class to learn."

"Name one who really wants to learn," I said.

He looked at me, then back at Mrs. Mendez, and went on: "It's been time wasted, all those chances, to no avail. I'm done using that approach with Chuy. It hasn't worked. So I want something done about this. And until something is done, I won't accept him back into my classroom."

Mrs. Mendez cleared her gargly throat and swallowed the gargajo. She looked at me and said, "And what's your side?"

I said, "Nothing." I knew their game. I'd say something, anything, right or wrong, and somehow I'd end up in more trouble than I was in already. Two weeks of in-school suspension versus two months. It was all the same to me. It was easy there; the coaches saw to it we were quiet and the cafeteria people brought us our trays of food. And like Mrs. Mendez really cared anyway. She was one of them, *the* one of them. They had each other's backs.

"You're not here in my office for 'nothing,'" she said. "If you don't speak up now, then I'll have to take Mr. Gutierrez's account as the final word. You could help yourself."

Or hurt myself, I thought. There it was—part of their plan—doomed if I did, doomed if I didn't. I decided to keep my mouth shut.

Except for Mr. G had to go and mess it up for me: "You're all about talking in the classroom, que eres un gangster pa'ca and that you're the tough guy pa'lla, and that ni Mrs. Mendez nor the cops can touch you, all big and tough in the class," he said. "Why won't you say anything now?—to her face, vato."

I freaked out. I'd never heard Mr. G talk like this; he'd always gone on proper and right and boring. This was something else.

"So?" asked Mrs. Mendez.

"Nothing at all," I said. "I don't know what bug crawled up Mr. G's butt and died."

"Excuse me?" she said.

Mr. G slapped at the armrest. "You see what I've got to put up with? I won't have any more of this."

And all of a sudden it was back to his old college-word-using self: "I expect you to act accordingly," he told Mrs. Mendez.

"I certainly will," she said. "Mr. Gutierrez, if you would step outside and fill out a referral. And get me copies of all the paperwork you've got on Chuy."

"Gladly, ma'am," he said, and left.

He shut the door behind him, and Mrs. Mendez was clicking away at her computer. I sat back to try to think things through. She wanted paperwork on me and she'd get plenty of it. If Mr. G was good at one thing, it was at keeping paperwork. He'd stop class in the middle of a lesson on the comma, or reading aloud; one time he stopped reading out of *Rumble Fish* just to write down that one of his students was misbehaving, and all the students booed him. He took his sweet time doing it, and since there was only one copy of the book, we had to wait for him to finish to get back to reading.

He'd stopped lessons because of me more times than I could count. I'd seen his journal once, the one he kept just for school things, and it was halfway filled with his notes: a date at the top, the time, a short title like "Chuy talking out of turn," and then a note. He always put the journal in his backpack when he was done.

"Chuy," said Mrs. Mendez, "why do you keep doing this? Getting in trouble, I mean? One of these days, you're going to cry wolf and no one's going to pay any attention to you."

"What?" I asked.

"If I know Mr. Gutierrez at all, I'm sure he's got plenty of notes on you, and I can't do anything to help you out if he's got everything documented. I see in my records," she said, and pointed at the computer screen in front of her, "that we've sent you to in-school suspension plenty already. Your days in there have run out. The next step, according to the rules, is a trip to the alternative center."

"What?" I said. "For talking when G's going on about something boring!"

"It's the next step," she said. "Rules are rules. You give us no way out. You've used up all the chances we can give."

"Listen, Miss," I said, and turned on the charm, "I swear, give me one more chance—ISS or after-school suspension, whatever—but one more chance, and I'll show you I can behave. I don't even have to be put into Mr. G's class. Send me to another teacher; Mr. Herrera, he's cool."

She looked like she was considering my idea, then said, "Chuy, I'll tell you what, let me think about this. Take a seat out there. In a few minutes I'll come out and tell you my decision."

"Thanks so much, Miss. You won't regret it."

I was talking to the secretary when Mr. G came

with his journal and started making copies, one page after another.

Mrs. Mendez called him into her office. "I'll talk to you in a bit, Chuy." She smiled a little, so I knew I'd talked her into letting me stay here and not sending me to the alternative center. Only the losers ended up there. I was no loser.

In a few moments, I heard the door open, Mr. G came out, shaking his head, and said, "I guess you won't need these copies, if that's your decision. Some system we've got going here. Perpetuating bad behavior. Wonderful!" he said. "It's a surprise so many of us stay at this job as long as we do." Then to me: "You are one lucky sonofagun. But you won't ever amount to much if you keep up this behavior. Good luck."

"Yeah, whatever, dude."

So she called me in next. "You won't be going to the alternative center. I'm counting on you, Chuy."

I nodded.

"Here's what's going to happen."

I listened, and inside I was all relieved. I'd have to help clean up the cafeteria after lunch, and I was going to be put in Mr. Herrera's class. My friends had told me he was easy, played the radio and let his students talk all the time.

"But this is your last chance," she said. "Appreciate what you're being given here."

"I do," I told her. Maybe I was wrong about her.

"Just wait outside for a few more minutes. I have to work out your schedule, okay?"

"Okay," I said, and sat down outside again.

I had started talking to the secretary when Mr. G came in huffing. He didn't even knock on Mrs. Mendez's door, just burst in on her and slammed it shut. I heard them shouting and all of us got quiet, me, the secretary, and the couple kids who had come in to hand in the attendance sheets. Something about "If this is how this district treats its teachers," then I don't know what else because Mrs. Mendez started yelling about how she was "the final word in this school" and she was "looking out for the welfare of her charges," and he said, "Speaking of charges, if nothing real is done to remedy this situation, I'll be calling my union rep and filing charges of my own."

Then Mr. G yanked the door open, walked out, I stood up, and he glared at me: "Happy?" he said.

"Siroles," I said. "I couldn't be happier."

But really, I felt bad because he was an okay guy and he had given me one chance after another, like the time when I pushed Lee up against the wall for hiding my notebook and Mr. G came to Lee's defense. He said, "Earlier in the day, if you remember right, Chuy, you took Lee's notebook and just tore a couple of sheets of his paper without asking. If you want him to respect your possessions, you have to respect his."

I screamed, "Tu me vales!" and all he did was look sad.

Instead of calling security for me cursing him in front of the whole class or writing me a referral, he sat down at his desk, all calm, then got up and went back to helping the other students with their work. Everyone was real quiet the rest of the hour, and nobody looked at me. G didn't even write me up in his journal. The next day I apologized to him, private, before class got started. Mrs. Mendez didn't have that one on her computer.

Today I also felt bad because the only other people I ever heard fighting were my parents, and then I just locked myself up in my room. Today G had screamed at Mrs. Mendez and she yelled at him. They both looked angry. I felt like crying, truth be told.

I called after Mr. G. He turned and said, "What do you want, Chuy? You want to spit in my face next?"

I said, "Ah, man, no way. I want to say I'm sorry. If you want, I can explain it to Mrs. Mendez."

"Explain what?" Mr. G asked, full up on me now. "That you don't care one iota for anyone but yourself? I thought you'd be happy now—I'll probably get fired for my little stunt, but you know what, I'll take full responsibility for my actions, unlike you."

"Man," I said, "I just want to try to fix this."

"How? Give her that famous smile of yours and then everything will be okay like it always is?" He walked out the door, and the door eased shut, slow, letting the heat from outside hit me in the face.

I heard Mrs. Mendez inside her office behind her door typing away, but real fast, like she didn't have enough time to type it all but she had to try.

I stood there in the leftover heat, my face just beginning to feel the cool of the air-conditioning. The door clicked shut, the secretary took a phone call, hung up, then knocked on Mrs. Mendez's door. She closed it behind her and I could hear one of them, maybe both of them, crying little baby cries. I imagined them holding each other, and I wished—never mind what I wished. Today I'd made Mrs. Mendez cry, and I'd probably gotten Mr. G fired—I was something else.

# 3

# SYLVIESYLVIESYLVIE

Sometimes it feels like I've got Pop Rocks going off real light in the right part of my head by the ear, but they get louder, moving to right smack between the eyes. They disappear for a few moments, sometimes they don't come back, but mostly they do after a few minutes, but the rocks are popping very light now and traveling in a line like ants across the back of my head and down my spine. Then I don't hear the popping. Sylvie calls them ants.

✦

Sylvie was a tiny girl. She was quiet, especially in school. She smiled and nodded every time the teacher said something that looked like he was going to call for some student participation. She'd learned that her teachers, most of them, called on students they knew would argue or answer wrong—to keep class going along on its merry way, Sylvie thought. The few words she spoke were to Randy, her boyfriend. They ate lunch together, just the two of them at a table, and the other kids poked fun at them, called them Mr. and Mrs. Special. "Hey, there's the Specials," they'd say, and laugh.

"Fools!" Randy'd say to Sylvie, and knock his fist once or twice against his head. "Idiots!"

Sylvie stayed quiet, except to say, "I can't eat. Finish my potatoes?"

Randy could hardly hear her, she thought, so she'd push her tray to him, and he'd get the picture and dig in.

Then they'd sit in silence.

✦

It hasn't happened to me in a while—the rocks popping—so I'm waiting on them any minute now. I'll just sit here with Sylvie and eat her mashed potatoes. It's like she can read my mind, knows when I haven't had enough. So she pushes her tray to me, smiles, says, Eat.

I eat, like she says. And wait for the rocks to come, loud, then light, then disappearing down my spine. It's been at least a couple days now.

✦

Sylvie was in English III now. Sitting, her journal open, drawing what she thought Randy's Pop Rocks looked like going through his head. Like ants. She had put that image in his mind. When he first told her how the rocks popping felt, he drew the back of his head and the little bubbles that exploded, all in lines, one behind the other. She'd said, "They're ants." Randy smiled and said, "Right, ants."

She was covering one page of her journal in a string

of ants, traveling down to the next line on the paper, across it left to right, then down a line and right to left. Half the page was covered.

Bobby stopped in front of her and said, "Hey, Mrs. Special, what you got going there?"

The others stopped talking and turned to look. Sylvie looked down at her journal. "Ants," she said.

"Ants?"

She nodded. Mr. Phillips was nowhere to be seen. Running late, as always. Probably talking to Miss Brecken, Sylvie thought, laughing his big teeth at her, touching her white forearm, squeezing it some like he always did.

Bobby snatched the journal.

She said, "Gimme it back."

"What's that, Mrs. Special? Gi' you back what? This?" Bobby held the journal open to the ants page, open like that in front of her face. "You want this back?"

She nodded.

"You'll have to take it."

She stood.

"Oooh, scary. Special's on the prowl." Bobby tore the ants page.

Sylvie took a step forward.

Bobby said, "But you'll get ants in your pants." He said, "Look," and pointed outside the window.

Sylvie turned to see what was outside the window he'd pointed to.

Then he pulled at her waistband and stuffed the

crumpled paper down her front. "Get it?" he said to the others. "Sylvie's got ants in her pants." They laughed.

"What's going on, Bobby?" asked Mr. Phillips.

Everyone stopped laughing. Bobby said, "Nothing," and put the journal back on her desk.

"Sylvie," said Mr. Phillips, "take a seat, please."

She sat. Sylvie'd never heard Bobby call her Sylvie, ever. It sounded nice coming out of his mouth, though.

She felt the crumpled-up paper scrunched and pressing on her, so she stuck her fingers down her pants carefully so no one would see and pulled it out. She smoothed the paper flat with her palm on her desk and replaced it in her journal. She smiled.

◆

Bobby kept looking over his right shoulder at Sylvie. She was looking down at her desk, writing something. Pink sparkly stars on her chest. Once, it seemed to Bobby she was making like she was turning her head, and, afraid to get caught looking, Bobby snapped his head forward and stared at the blackboard. He'd stare at the board instead, he thought, at all his teacher's chicken scratch; that way he wouldn't have to look at Sylvie. And why was he so obsessed with looking at her? She was Mrs. Special, hair all knotted up and no hips to speak of, sometimes she wore makeup, smeared like she'd let a retard put it on her. He'd never paid any attention to her, really, except to poke fun at her, call her names, laugh at her and her boyfriend. But today he needed to look at her. She was different to him. Today.

Earlier, when he had pulled on the front of her pants, Sylvie had looked scared, but after a second, she looked him in the eyes and didn't seem afraid anymore. And it seemed to him she let him reach down her front where he stuffed the crumpled paper. He had pulled his fingers out fast, then had to say something to clear up the red he could feel coming up his neck, a pulsating red that locked itself on his face, pounding at his temples. So he made a stupid joke—Sylvie had ants in her pants—the others laughed, Mr. Phillips walked in and screamed at them to shut up. Sylvie had smiled at him, though. Right there at the end, when he was turning to walk to his desk, she had smiled.

Then he was at his desk, fighting the urge to turn and look at her. What was with the smile? he wondered. Had she liked it—me putting my hand down her pants? Was she like Mary, loose and quick to kiss on a first date, and then let you touch her all over? Bobby didn't want Sylvie to be like that.

But why? Bobby didn't want to be that sort of guy, either, one who touched her, then touched her a second time, then word'd get out and that would be the end for her, the girl with the bad rep. He thought, It could be an improvement, though.

But why did it matter to him about her? He looked again. She was still writing. What could she be writing? He wanted to know real bad. He would call her aside in the hall, somewhere no one would notice them, maybe behind the lockers by the art lab, and apologize for what he'd done. She'd say, That's okay or something. Then he'd ask what she'd been writing the whole time in class, "It couldn't've been notes on Mr. Phillips's lecture." He'd chuckle, and she'd touch his arm. "No," she'd answer, "but if you really want to know—" She'd pull the notebook from her backpack and show it to him: "I love Bobby! I love Bobby!" it would say, page after page, little hearts around the name Bobby. "Mr. and Mrs. Bobby." Then he'd say, "I love you, too," and they'd hold hands walking down the hallway, everybody looking at them but no one laughing. She was Bobby's girl now, not Randy's, not Mrs. Special anymore, but Mrs. Bobby.

Then he shook his head clear. What was he thinking? It was crazy. He was crazy. She was Mrs. Special. He had to get over having to look at her, had to stop thinking about her this way. She was still a freak.

✦

"So, what are you going to do about it?" someone asks. I don't know who; I don't care who. "I mean, Bobby just put his hand down her pants and touched her thing, man. You going to let that go? Stand back and ignore it, like he never did nothing to her?"

I grab my collar and bunch it up in my right hand. I don't want to whack at my head, because that would mean the Pop Rocks, the crawling ants. "No," I say. I walk away from whoever and look for Sylvie. She's out in the garden in front of the library, so I ask her, "D'you like it? When Bobby touched you? Like this?"

"Stop it, Randy."

"So you did like it? No one told me you said, Stop it, to Bobby."

"Please, stop," she says, and cries.

I pull my hand away. I don't like it when girls cry.

I pull my hand away and sit on the bench.

Sylvie leaves, and in my head there's *a boy, third grade, maybe fourth?*

*One of the boy's hands, his tiny bunched-up fist, clutching his green sweatshirt at the neck. The other hand, flat and rubbing at his chest and stomach. Crying. Wah! Wah! Wah! Silencing, in his own way, his mother's screaming and beating on his sisters: Whores! The both of you! Whack! Whack! Releasing his sweatshirt, the boy begins banging on the side of his head, loosing the Pop Rocks, shaking them loose, knocking on the insides of his skull.* Pop pop crackle. *Slithering to the back of his head, then down his spine. Banging on his head to stop the screaming.*

◆

"Hey, Sylvie," says Bobby. She's walking down the hall, toward the bus pickup. She turns. "Hey, wait up."

She stops.

"About today," he says. "I'm sorry. I shouldn't've did what I did."

She stands there in front of him, quiet.

"Well?" he says. "Am I forgiven?"

She's holding her journal up to her chest. She means to say, Oh, don't worry about it, it's okay, but before she can speak, Bobby asks, "During class, in your notebook there"—and he points to it—"what were you writing?"

"This?"

"Yes," he says.

She shakes her head. "Oh, nothing," but before she can say she'd been writing her name, all curvy, all covered in little flowers and leaves, her name covering a whole page, then on the next page her name over and over, no blank space left open: SylvieSylvieSylvie— before she can say that, she's shoved aside: "Whoa!" she says.

"Apologize!" says Randy, all in Bobby's face.

"Get out of my face, freak!"

"Apologize!" He's grabbing at his collar, squishing it in a tight fist. The Pop Rocks are coming.

"I said, get out of my face, or else." The red is climbing up the back of Bobby's neck, and up to his face.

Randy whacks himself on the side of the head.

"What's up with that, freak?"

Then Bobby gets it in the nose, and there's blood all down the front of his shirt, and he drops to one knee. He's not thinking about Sylvie having written in her journal, I love Bobby! I love Bobby! Instead, he's seeing black behind his closed eyes, and stars, itty-bitty ones, first crawling, then shooting toward him, and he wonders should he duck, get out of the stars' way?

A crowd gathers. "What's going on here?" asks the security guard. "Someone go get me some paper towels." Then he calls for the nurse and backup on his walkie-talkie. More guards show up, ask students some questions—"Who? Him?"—and a guard takes Randy off to one of their gray cars. He sits in the backseat, still. The ants have come and gone. He looks down at his fist and wipes Bobby's blood on his pants.

Bobby's laid out on the grass, the nurse pressing an ice bag to his face. He's calm in the shade under a tree. Only his right foot keeps tapping at the air. He's thinking, All for a girl? Not even!

Sylvie sees her bus approaching, looks at Bobby, then at Randy, walks to catch her bus, and thinks, SylvieSylvieSylvie. That just sounds so right.

Mark had never been in a play before, not even at church, where the pastor told him that all he had to do for the Christmas play was stand beside Mandy, hold a staff, and look down at the Baby Jesus. "Just tie a towel around your head," the pastor said, "and be Joseph. Joseph doesn't speak a word." Back then, Mark hadn't liked the idea, so this morning when he had to fill out his electives card to hand in to his counselor, he didn't know why he wrote in "Drama." But he did.

Next morning when he picked up his schedule, he saw he'd been put into Mr. Simonton's seventh-period drama class. Mark felt his breakfast jumble in his stomach a little bit. He'd heard Mr. Simonton was new, and he was black.

When the bell rang for seventh period, Mark leaned against the wall opposite the drama room and cased the place. Two girls were already in class, talking to Mr.

Simonton. He was laughing, sitting behind his desk. And he was black.

A few other students walked in, mostly girls at first, but then a few guys went in and Mark walked in behind them. Everyone took their seats when the tardy bell rang, and Mr. Simonton introduced himself and passed out a calendar of events for the first semester. Mark read they'd be doing a lot of in-class acting, nothing major. Then he heard Mr. Simonton say, "Now, if you turn the sheet over, you'll see how after we're done with all this prep work, we'll be working toward a big Christmas show. Then, if you decide to stick it out for a second semester, we'll begin practice for the district competition."

Mark wasn't thinking that far ahead yet. He didn't even know if he'd stick it out another day, what with "Being a tree" and "Breathing exercises," and worse, the project, "The Twelve Days of Christmas."

"You're in the wrong place if you thought this was going to be an easy A," said Mr. Simonton.

The following days, all they did in drama class was talk, and a few of the others volunteered to do "angry" and "horrified" and "sad" in front of the class. Mark was very impressed by Debbie. She was one of the only white kids in the school, and she could act. Mark felt a lump in his throat when Debbie's bottom lip began to quiver, and then when she began to really cry, boy, he wanted to get up and hug her. Then she cut off the tears, said thank you, bowed, and sat down while the rest of the class applauded. Mark decided he'd stick it out. At least for the rest of this semester.

Two weeks in, Mr. Simonton kicked out two boys and a girl because they "weren't working out," he told the class. "You've got to toe the line, baby," he said. "This acting business, it isn't an easy thing. It's serious, and it can get you places."

Two weeks after that, he called Miguel out into the hallway, and Mark could hear them yelling: "I'm sick and tired of your attitude," said Mr. Simonton.

"And I'm sick and tired of you, period!" screamed Miguel.

"That's it. You're out," said Mr. Simonton.

"You don't got to tell me twice. Your class sucks anyways. You call yourself an actor. What TV you ever been on?" Miguel was probably the best actor in the class, but he'd taken to memorizing lines for a skit so-so, no real energy behind them like Mr. Simonton required. A week before, Miguel had whispered to the others that Mr. Simonton had no clue what he was doing, that an actor friend of his from another school had said, "My director, when I told him what you all are doing in class, he laughed and said, 'That's not acting. Oh well, that's one less team we have to worry about beating at the district meet.'"

Miguel didn't come back in, and it took Mr. Simonton a few minutes of pacing before he did. He was fuming. "There's the door," he said from behind his desk. He pointed at the open door. "Get out if you're not going to take this seriously. This is no game. No one makes fun of my vocation. If you're staying, then there's no namby-pamby baby attitudes. Got it?" He waited a few moments, and when no one got up to leave, he got back to his serious business. "Good! Now let's get busy."

All that semester, Mr. Simonton trained the class in trusting one another: "Because out onstage, each other's all you got." One exercise called for one person to fall backward, having faith that his partner would catch him before hitting the ground. Debbie and Mark were partners. When it was her turn, she looked at him over her shoulder and said, "Don't you let me fall."

Mark smiled. "Trust me, I'm a doctor."

"Whatever. Just make sure and catch me."

He did catch her. She felt so soft in his arms. She stood and said, "Your turn."

He said, "I'm trusting you." He smiled.

"Whatever, sure." She didn't drop him, but he didn't feel soft in her arms, more like a sack of potatoes.

Mr. Simonton also liked to play his records. He introduced the class to Prince. Mr. Simonton sang along to "When Doves Cry" and "1999." Everybody joined in, even Mark, who didn't like the sound of his own voice.

In November, for the school's talent show, Mr. Simonton and Debbie lip-synched "Ebony and Ivory" by Stevie Wonder and Paul McCartney. They wore T-shirts that looked like tuxedos, and Mr. Simonton wore sunglasses and fake played the piano. When he swung his head back and forth and smiled, he looked just like Stevie Wonder, and everyone in the audience laughed and clapped. They won lunch at the snack bar.

A few days after the talent show, Mr. Simonton said, "It's time to start practicing for the Christmas show. We'll be performing for the three elementary schools. We'll do a few skits, but the grand finale will be us acting out 'The Twelve Days of Christmas.'" They had three after-school practices a week for a month and a half.

Maybe it was just that they'd be getting out of classes for two full days to go sing a song to the kiddies in the school district, or maybe Mark had worked through some of his fears of speaking in front of groups of strangers, but he had no qualms about wearing baby-blue pj's with a little bunny on the front, making like he was a gold ring, a drummer boy, a maid a-milking. I'll be part of the group, he thought. I won't be alone.

December arrived and they played to several hundred kids to huge success. Standing ovations all around. Cheering. Clapping. Stomping of little feet, and laughing. And hugs after, when they all helped tear down the set. Simonton kept them an hour and a half after school for another practice. "I noticed some parts we need to work on. It's got to be dead-on."

Debbie said, "Aw, come on, S, they're only kids. What do they know?"

Simonton turned and left the stage. A few seconds later he came back and screamed, "They are an audience. *Your* audience! If you think you can let it slide because they're snot-nosed kids, then you're the ignorant ones," and he looked right at Debbie, who was staring at the floor. "Listen," he said a few seconds later, "sorry, it just pi— I get upset when you guys think acting is a joke. It's a job like any other, and an art besides, so you have to be disciplined. You've got to push yourselves." He had tears in his eyes. Mark wanted to cry too. "So let's get this thing right."

At the end of the second day, the troupe of actors returned to the high school, where Mr. Simonton said, "Okay, much better. And, Debbie, way to keep the rest of us on track during the five gold rings. Hey, since we've got plenty of time left in the school day, and it'd be a shame to waste your talent, what do you think, let's go down the halls and see who'll let us put on our show?"

"Chale, Simonton," said one of the boys. "No way I'm singing in front of the vatos here."

"I don't get it," the teacher said. "You just sang in front of hundreds of kids for the past two days. What's the big deal?"

"This is in front of people who know us. That's a big difference."

"Listen," said Simonton, "I know what you're feeling. You'll goof up in front of your friends, they'll laugh maybe. But what does that matter? You guys are actors. Good ones."

"Sorry, Simonton, but chale."

"Oh, come on, guys. Listen, you don't even have to wear the pajamas. Just sing."

"No'mbre, vato," said one of them, "they'll think we're sissies."

"No way, Simonton. Sorry," said Debbie.

Mark felt bad. They were letting their teacher down, the one who had, more than any other teacher, treated them with respect all this time, who had showed them for the first time what it meant to be adults. He had placed responsibility on their shoulders, had told them, "Nothing's there to stop you: be successful." Mark wanted to say something, but he didn't.

"If that's your answer," Mr. Simonton said, "then let's all go to the office. I won't stand for this insubordination."

"¿Que's insubordination?" one of them whispered.

Mark didn't know what the word meant either, but he'd look it up. He knew it wasn't good, though. They just sat at their desks.

"Every one of you," said Mr. Simonton, "to the office. Now!"

"Are you joking?" Debbie asked.

"I'm not. Let's go."

He walked his group to the assistant principal, La Tweety, students called her, but never to her face. And never out of disrespect. She was on the tiny side, her face like a cartoon character's. Her glasses always seemed to be hanging off the edge of her nose ready to fall, but they never did. Also, only the cool principals

INSTRUCTIONAL MEDIA CENTER
GRISSOM MIDDLE SCHOOL
MISHAWAKA, INDIANA

got nicknames that started with El or La. La Tweety
would yell when students needed yelling, she'd talk
soft and offer a shoulder when they needed that.

This time she said, "Whoa, whoa! What's going
on?" There were twelve days of Christmas in her eight-
by-eight office.

"Mr. Simonton sent us here. Miss, he wants to
make us sing in front of the school. That's so embarrassing," said Debbie. The others nodded.

Mr. Simonton crammed in behind them, standing
just inside the door. "Mrs. Garza," he said, "I want to
report all of these kids for being insubordinate." There
was that word again. Mark tried to spell it out in his
head so he wouldn't forget it. It was obvious that La
Tweety knew what it meant, and she shook her head
and pursed her lips. Maybe something like disrespect,
thought Mark.

"You kids go and wait in the hall," she said.

"Pero, Miss—" started one of the boys.

"Don't give me any of that. Go wait in the hall. Mr.
Simonton and I need to talk in private."

They all squished through the door and hung out in
the hallway. Some of the guys said all kinds of bad
things about Mr. Simonton, and some of the girls even
started to say halfway bad things about La Tweety, so
that if she sided with him they'd have a head start on
cursing her.

After a few minutes, Mr. Simonton came out and
asked them all to pile back into Tweety's office.

"Now," Tweety said, "Mr. Simonton tells me he

wanted you to sing to a few classes only, not the *whole* school. He understands about you being embarrassed to perform in front of your peers, but that's nothing more than an excuse. He tells me you all are very good, and he just wanted to show off your talent. But you refused." She looked at them over her glasses. "I told him he couldn't force you to do this because I don't want you to go into a classroom and not do your best. That would be something to be truly embarrassed about. So, he's going to give you an F for the assignment."

No one said anything.

"But I'll have you know, both Mr. Simonton and I are very disappointed in you. You're supposed to be the leaders on campus. We're disappointed, yes. Well, I've got some paperwork to get to, so go back to class now, don't make a peep on the way there or else you'll get in school suspension for three days. When you get to class, I want you to think about what you've done, and what it all means."

They followed Mr. Simonton back to their room. No one made a sound. Mark was too busy looking down at the floor. He shook his head in disgust. Why hadn't he told the rest of them, Okay, if you won't do it, fine, but I'm with Mr. Simonton? Instead, he'd stood back and looked down in front of him and said nothing. Like he was doing now.

Mr. Simonton unlocked the door, stepped aside, and let the students in. A few seconds after they'd gotten settled, he sat behind his desk and didn't say a word.

"Sir," said Debbie.

He lifted his head and glared at her.

"Sir?"

"What!"

"Well, I'm sorry about the mess. If you still want to go, I'll go with you."

"Yeah, me too," said one of the boys.

Mark's legs were shaking, and in his throat he felt the words coming. They were there: "Yeah, count me in," or "Yeah, I got your back, Mr. Simonton." But he didn't speak. He just shook his legs and looked down at a drawing of a cat etched onto his desk. Then he looked up.

Mr. Simonton bit his bottom lip, then said, "It's too late for that."

# 5

## ANDY AND RUTHIE

At this place in the story, it's a long time ago, when Andy first moved with his family to Mission. On his first day in the fifth grade, he eats his lunch alone, then leaves the cafeteria. He stands off to the side of the playground, all to himself, under the shade of a mesquite tree, looking down at the dirt.

Some boys walk up to him and say things like "Hey, it's the new kid" and "What's his name, d'ya think?" and "New kid, what's your name?"

"Andy."

Then one of them, not even the biggest of the bunch, bumps into him and says, "Hey, funny hair, watch where you're stepping," and whacks him on the head.

"But I didn't."

He gets whacked again. "Didn't you hear him say you did, Andy the Funny-Haired Freak? Watch your step. Or else."

Then they make a circle around him and all jump on him, six boys all shoving and whacking Andy.

Then he hears "Hey!"

The six boys stop going at Andy with their closed fists and turn to see who's screamed at them. It is Ruthie, a fourth grader. One of them walks up to her and says, "Go on, snot-nose. Can't you see we're busy here, playing with Andy? Or do you want some of this too?"

"I'm not stupid," she says.

"That's right," he says, and grabs her shoulder to turn her around. "Because if you were, you'd stick around and get some of this for yourself."

With her fist, a little ball of bone, Ruthie smashes his mouth and there's blood, a little at first on his fingers where he rubbed, then a lot, running down the front of his shirt. The boy's knees buckle and he crumples. The others pick up their friend, who's like a scarecrow, all wobbly and wiping the blood from his mouth and crying. "What you do that for, huh?"

They all walk away holding up their friend, still all wobbly in the legs.

Now it's two years later; Andy had to be without Ruthie day in, day out for a whole year last year when he moved on to middle school and she stayed in elementary. But now it's okay. It's the first day of a new year and they get off their different buses and meet over by the cafeteria, right where they planned to meet last night on the phone. This morning Ruthie looks nervous, and says so.

"It's nothing to be worried about," says Andy. "Things'll be good. You'll get used to it, you'll see. And we're together again." He doesn't tell her that he did not sleep all night, anxious about another year of school, about being beat up by the big kids or poked fun at, but at least they're together again, and that helps. This morning he's still wound up, but not so much as last night. "You want to go to the office to get our schedules?"

"Yeah," she says.

Now it's a year later. Andy's not doing so well in eighth grade. His teachers, his counselor, and his parents all say, "We don't get it; last year he was an A student. College track."

His parents talk to him: "Is it drugs?" they ask, and keep a close eye on him the rest of the semester.

He tells them, "No, it's not drugs; classes have just all of a sudden got hard for me."

But his parents go through his things, "to be on the safe side," they say when he catches them. "Better you hate us now for this; later, when you're grown, you'll know how much we love you."

But things don't improve. His parents just don't get it, and he fails every one of his classes and has to repeat the year.

This way, Ruthie's all caught up.

———

Now it's their senior year in high school. Andy's getting ready to ask Ruthie to prom. They've been going steady for three years, and all the teachers say, "First thing they'll do after they're both graduated is get married and have three kids." But that's not what either of them wants. Not right off the bat, anyway. They both want to go to college, get degrees, he in architecture and she in prelaw. They've got grand plans. A wedding too early would mean kids too soon would mean taking longer to finish college, if at all.

Finally Andy figures he's waited long enough to ask her to prom. Last week, talking with Ruthie, he said, "Hey, after the dance, where do you want to go eat?"

She said, "What dance?"

"Prom, silly."

"I haven't been asked to no prom."

"It's understood, ain't it?" he said. "We're boyfriend-girlfriend."

"Maybe in Andylandia, but in Ruthie's World a boy's still got to ask his girl, no matter how understood it is."

Andy got up from the table and took her tray. "Is that so?"

"Yeah."

He left to dump the trays. The bell rang and they walked to their next class. She dropped him off at his door. "Well, are you going to ask?"

"I'll think about it."

"Not too long," she said.

———

Now Andy's come up with a good plan to ask her. At first he was mad at her. She should have known it was understood, like he said. It's always understood he doesn't have to ever ask to carry her books. He just takes them and she lets him. But maybe this is different. She's going to need a dress. Even though the one she wore to his sister's wedding two months ago would work. He guesses that a girl just likes to be asked. Then he has to do it right.

He waits for her to join him for lunch at their table. He says, "Oh, let's finish eating. I have to get something from our locker." He smiles down at his plate because of his master plan. She's going to love it, he thinks, and smiles more. He sees Ruthie's not smiling. She will be, though.

They walk over to the locker. He sticks his hands in his backpack and is pretending to fiddle with something in there, so he says, "Do me a favor, can you open that?"

Ruthie turns the knob this way that way and back. She jerks open the locker and a balloon halfway pops out. It's a big pink heart with little red hearts painted all around. "What could this be?" he asks, smiling big, standing next to Ruthie now. "Who could've put that in there? Pull it out and see."

There's a card on the end of the string. She opens it, reads the note, then slaps him.

Now he's on the phone with her that night, trying to figure out why the slap: that time of the month, maybe? Didn't he do right by her to ask her all fancy like he did, a balloon, a note, like a big show?

"So what was up with you?"

"Two weeks. You waited two weeks—fourteen days, fifteen, actually, from when we talked last about this—and it's only one week till prom."

"I didn't know there was a time frame, that I had to read your mind."

"Don't get smart on me."

"Don't you get all sassy."

"Sassy?" she asks.

"Yeah, because I don't know how to read your mind and I don't know what you're thinking. So, I've asked. Now, what time will I pick you up? And I'll forget all about the slap."

"You waited too long, Andy. Jonny asked me a month ago, and I waited as long as I could for you to ask, but you never did, so I'm going with Jonny."

"But—but we're boyfriend-girlfriend."

Now it's prom night. All this time he hasn't let on to his parents he and Ruthie aren't going to prom together. When his dad asked earlier in the week if he needed some money for a corsage, or for food, Andy said, "No, I got plenty, but thanks. I would like to use the car, though." He was going to play it all the way through. To keep his parents from asking too many questions and then thinking Ruthie's cheating on their son with another boy, all the while stringing their Andrew along. When he was moping that week and they asked him about it, he said, "Oh, it's nothing. Maybe the flu," and his mom checked his forehead with a cold hand and said, "You don't feel warm, but to be on the safe side, go to bed early tonight. Might be one of those twenty-four-hour bugs." So he did, and cried a little. His dad checked on him when he got home from work, but Andy made like he was sleeping and couldn't hear his father asking, "You okay, son?"

The next day, Andy's dad gives him the keys to the car and twenty dollars. "Get those guys downtown to wash it. Don't take it to the gas station through the automatic wash. That scratches the side panels all up. Fifteen's for the wash, the other five for a tip. It's important to tip big. That way they'll take extra good care of you the next time. Shake their hands, too." Andy takes the keys, pockets the money, and leaves. He waits for the car to get washed.

Out front, a guy honks a horn. Andy's car's ready. He pays and says, "No. Keep the change," but forgets to shake the guy's hand. He leaves to pick up his tuxedo. When he gets home, his mom wants to take a picture or two of him dressed up: "Oh, our little boy's all grown now," she says.

Now he's sitting in his dad's car in the school gymnasium's parking lot. He's got the windows rolled down and the radio on, but he can't stand listening. Every song that comes on is a slow song and he imagines him and Ruthie dancing tight and close, the smell of her perfume, her fruity hair spray. So he shuts off the radio and bangs his fist on the dash. Andy can see red green and blue lights flashing every time someone opens the doors to go in or out of prom. They arrive all dressed up and walk to the gym arm in arm, the guys being so gentleman-like and opening the door for their girls. Andy whacks the dash again. There're also snippets of music when the doors open, then close. "I waited too long," he says to himself, and punches at the dash. This time is the last because he's left a ding on it.

It's two hours later, and Andy's been out in his car all this while. People begin to file out, first a few couples, then none, then a whole bunch. He's looking for Ruthie and Jonny. His plan's simple: when Jonny and Ruthie get in their car, he'll go to the burger joint and order something to go, eat in the park slow, take an hour or so, then a half hour more sitting there so his parents won't catch on. Then go home after, not too early. That's his plan, but it turns out Jonny's car is only two down from his, and even though he tries to slide down in his seat, Ruthie sees him and says, "Andy, is that you? What are you doing here? Who'd you come with?"

Andy waves at her goodbye but she comes over to him. She's wearing the dress she wore to his sister's wedding. Her hair's curly, and in the light her face and shoulders sparkle with fairy dust.

He's crying a little, and says, "I didn't come. I've been sitting here all night. I didn't tell my parents we weren't going. They think I'm out with you right now, their little boy all grown up, so I didn't want to disappoint them."

By now Jonny's come up and heard what Andy's said, and laughs, "What a loser, man." He turns to tell a couple of his buddies who have congregated around his car. They laugh too.

"I just wanted so much to go with you, but I messed up, Ruthie. I'm sorry."

"It's okay. Listen, I have to finish my date tonight. He's not at all what I thought he'd be. Truth be told, he's boring. You wouldn't think so, him being part of the football team and National Honor Society. But he's not smart at all, and I wonder why he's in NHS. And—" But Jonny interrupts her.

"We going or what?" he says. "My crew's waiting. Just tell freakshow here bye-bye, and let's get a move on. I'm hungry."

"I'll call you," she says, and turns to go.

Andy nods.

"Later, crybaby," says Jonny.

Ruthie stops.

Jonny says, "Shake a leg, will you?"

Then he walks back to get her, and she says, "No. You go on ahead."

"What?"

"I said—"

"I heard what you said. What I meant is that I ain't going alone to dinner. I paid for your flowers, I made reservations, and I'm expecting you to come. What're your options, anyway? Go home with loserboy over there?"

"Sure, why not?"

"Because he's a loser, and you'll be one too if you don't come with me right now. You want that? I can help you, or I can hurt you with your rep. So what's it going to be? Me, or freakshow?"

Andy has heard every word, and now can see Ruthie's fingers ball up into a fist: "I'm going with my boyfriend," she says, "and you're the freakshow."

"You're a waste of time and money," Jonny says.

That's when she pops him on the mouth.

ALTERNATIVE

For this to work, you've got to back off, give me a little bit of storytelling room, especially when you start thinking what I'm telling you isn't making so much sense, like a story should you'd read in a book. It won't be at all exciting and action-packed like *The Count of Monte Cristo;* or scary like Edgar Allan Poe's stories (I'm thinking about the one where there's the heart beating somewhere under that guy's house and he can't figure out where from); or about love and death like in *Romeo and Juliet,* not even like in the movie with that skinny punk DiCaprio, who all the girls at school fall totally in love with.

Because this is what Mr. Ramirez, my all-day teacher at the Alternative Center, calls autobiography, or personal narrative. En otras palabras, it's got to be true what I tell about myself. Mr. Ramirez says we've all got a story, "And if you look hard enough," he says, "you'll see you have many more to tell."

I've got nothing but time here in the Center, where I was sent about a month ago. So I'll give it a try.

Most of us in the Center are the ones teachers don't want in the classrooms no more. Los losers. The football coach calls us pedazos de—number two. I'm trying to keep it clean here, but I want my gringa counselor at the Center to understand how things go for us out there.

I'm writing about how I ended up at the Alternative Center. It was drugs. That, plus I don't like people talking about my mother. No me dejo. I mean, I don't take you-know-what from nobody, not even my teachers. Not even Mr. Sifuentes, my teacher back at the high school. He tries to be cool with us, old as he is, using words like "vato," "ese," and "trucha." He says he comes from the same barrios as we're from, but what does he know about our barrios today? He says, "The only difference between you and me, in that respect, is about twenty years and computers; it's all in the technology," he says. "You play on Sega; I played on Atari. You have better technology is all. Otherwise, somos iguales."

But the dude never answered our questions about what drugs he did, or does, or does he drink, and party? Did he ever get into fights? What gang does he belong to, or belonged to back in the day? He just says, "None of that's important. You're asking the wrong questions. You're trying to look at the wrong person. You should be asking, Where did you study? How'd you get out? Why are you back? Who are you right now?"

That's what I'm saying in my story too. Look at where I'm at right now. I'm not in my regular classes no more, not for the rest of the semester.

All because of Mr. Sifuentes. About three months back, we started reading *The Count of Monte Cristo*. He told us this story had it all, more than anything we'd see at the movies: action, prison, escape, death, murder, love, and revenge. I liked it okay, but some of it was just too slow, so I'd put my head down. Some days Mr. Sifuentes would be reading, or San Juanita would be, and then Sifuentes would ask a question. When no one would answer, he'd say, joking, "Too bad Turo's asleep; otherwise, he'd be able to answer." I'd open my eyes then and give him the answer, and he'd say, "Man, even asleep you're smart." Sifuentes was a good guy. Every time I'd show up late because I was still eating my lunch or whatever, he'd say, "You need to try getting to class on time, Arturo," and he'd pat me on the back. "Orale," I always told him. But he never reported me. He'd let us go to the snack machines during class if we were still hungry. Not all the time, but sometimes. Bien trucha el guy.

But this one day, just over a month ago, I came in, and to tell the truth I was a little doped up (and here I'm trusting Mr. Ramirez when he said, "Tell the truth for the sake of the story. You won't get in trouble, no matter what.") I'd been hanging out with some vatos who I knew were maybe more than I could handle. Dudes who were dropouts or about to drop out. Vatos who said they'd broken into houses and stolen all kinds of junk to sell, or for fun. Vatos who always had a Baggie of this or that with them, willing to share, and tattoos across their backs in Old English letters. Guys who would look a cop in the eye and not show fear, or hate, or nothing. Completely blank, no matter what trouble they were in. Gangsters to the core.

I wasn't part of the gang yet. I didn't want to be, and they never said I should be. We just hung out, and I started smoking dope.

Anyway, back to the story: that day, I came in sleepy and out of it. Y worse, I came in late, and I was floating. I'm telling you, I was high like the clouds. Came in eating sunflower seeds. I had them all bunched up in my right fist and spilling half of them. I walked right in front of Mr. Sifuentes, who was already into his reading: "Glad you could join us, Arturo."

"Glad to be here," I said, and laughed, dropping all kinds of seeds, and headed to my desk at the back of the room. I put my head down, and Mr. Sifuentes didn't get back to his reading. He was talking, but I wasn't understanding what he was saying to me. He was too far away, way in front of the classroom and behind his desk, standing, pointing to the floor to his left. Then it hit me he was talking to me: "Pick up your mess, Arturo. Come on, you made it, now clean it up."

"We got janitors for that, ese," I said, and Osvaldo next to me laughed.

"We do, but their job is not to be picking up after you. Now come up and clean up your mess."

"They're seeds, vato. Environmentally friendly."

Osvaldo laughed again. "Clean them up yourself if they bother you."

"I would, but I'm not your mother to be cleaning up after you."

That's when I blew my top. "What'd you say about my mother? Nobody, and I mean nobody, talks bad about my mother!" I said, and threw all the seeds on the floor. I got up screaming, "What'd you say about my mother, dude?" All the time walking up to the front and shoving desks aside; I even turned one over, and Mr. Sifuentes screaming right back, "I didn't say anything about your mother. I said I'm not your mother." He stood his ground, even with me rushing up front like I was, a piece of chalk between his fingers, twirling it, and looking at me, but not coming out from behind the desk. I cursed him, if I remember right. Said he could go you-know-where, that if he ever talked about my mother again, I'd beat the living you-know-what out of him. That's when he said, "Forget the seeds, and forget you! Get out of my room, and don't ever, ever! come back." Now he was out from behind his desk, and I'm walking out of the room. I slammed the door behind me, still cursing at him. Teachers were sticking their fat heads out their doors, and shutting them quickly. Mr. Sifuentes flung open his door and came out after me, screaming too. By then security had shown up. Probably one of those teachers hiding behind their closed doors buzzed for them to come— "And hurry, we've got a lunatic out in the hall yelling at the top of his lungs."

All the time I'm freaking out because Sifuentes wasn't hiding behind his door. Was right behind me, his chest puffed out, and in his eyes a look: I'm ready to go at it with you, just say the word.

Security caught up with me and had me sit in the office. Later, one of them brought a pretty long referral, from Mr. Sifuentes, I guess. Hey, I wasn't going down this easy, though. The dude had talked about my mother, and that's just not done. I explained this to the principal the next morning when my mother showed up with me for a discipline meeting, and my mom looked at me all funny and said, "I wish you'd clean your room with the same passion that you're defending my honor, then the house would be spotless."

"Tu no sabes nada," I told her, holding my own.

"I know more than you think. I know this isn't about me and my honor, it's about you being stupid."

I shut it off then. She and the principal were talking about I don't know what; and that's when I knew I wasn't going to have it easy anymore, when my mother said, "Do what you have to with him. I'm done getting him out of trouble. He needs to learn life ain't easy. What papers do I have to sign?"

I'm shaking my head the whole time and huffing, but neither of them paid me any attention, like I wasn't even there, so I walked out. I heard the principal screaming after me, then the security guard who was sitting just outside his office got in my way and I shoved him aside, and he grabbed me by the wrist in one of those karate locks they're always talking about, and I don't mind telling you, it hurt and I couldn't do anything to get out of it. Then the cops came, and I fought them when one each grabbed me by the arms. I got free of one of them and kicked at the other, then it was all over. I was down on the floor breathing in pavement, with the sting of one of their knees in my back, and cuffed.

And here I am, a month later, in the Alternative Center, the last stop before the Camps in San Benito. They're the last last stop. I heard about the Camps from a dude who got here a week after me. Then he's gone one day, all of a sudden; his head shaved clean and eyes like the dudes I was hanging out with before all my troubles started. All empty. He said it's physical training the whole day, and classes taught by ex-marines, and if you step out of line, it's more exercise in the yard, where it's all sand, so jogging in place or running sprints is harder that way. Sand all in your mouth doing push-ups. And the marine dudes screaming at you the whole entire time. Chale.

So I'm trying to straighten up. Mr. Ramirez says write a personal narrative, and here it is, but this isn't the whole story.

There's more to it. The other day, la secretary came and found me at lunch and handed me a bag from Desert Bloom Bookstore. Inside the bag I found copies of *Monte Cristo, Cross and the Switchblade,* and a note from Mr. Sifuentes. It says, "Arturo: I am sorry that we got into it like we did. I didn't mean to offend you when I brought up your mother, but when you said what you

said about janitors, you were talking about my grandfather, and other people's fathers and mothers. Janitors are also people, and are also mothers. Not yours,
but somebody's. Anyway, I apologize, and hope the
best for you. By the way, you never got to finish *The
Count of Monte Cristo,* so here's your own copy, and another book that helped me out when I was your age.
There are other ways out. Read them and tell me what
you think. Orale, Mr. Sifuentes."

I haven't finished either of the books, but I will.
Hopefully by the end of my time here. I won't go visit
the dude, but he's all right, I guess. The vato apologized. He's got to be big to do that.

So this is it, my autobiography. My story. I don't see
that it's a good story. I mean, there's no trick ending,
no happy ending, no ending period that I can point to.
I'm still here, ain't I?

There's no love in it either. No pretty girls; al-
though San Juanita's pretty, but you see how I didn't
go into her as part of the story. She's dating someone
serious, and I think I heard someone say she was preg-
nant, but that's not my story, it's hers. If she wants to
tell it, fine.

Reading over this, I don't see any action, and no
moral. Mr. Ramirez said, "And let the story end where
it ends. What's the last thing that happens? What's the
last thing someone says that's important in the story?
Don't ride off into the sunset. Don't give us a lesson to
learn, the moral, that is. Smart readers can figure that
out for themselves."

It just doesn't feel right to finish like this. Maybe I've gone on too long. I hope this ending doesn't get me a failing grade. I mean I've checked and rechecked the spelling, looked at the grammar and periods and commas. So here it is.

Oh, let me throw in a poem I also wrote, another of Mr. Ramirez's assignments from when I first got to the Center. Here goes:

### Ain't Nothing nor Nobody

I ain't your mother, he said.
No you ain't, I said, wanting to knock him in
    the head.
You ain't nothing to me, I said.
That's fine, he said, but you ain't got nothing
    in your head.
I bunch up my fist
And want to knock him in the head
So bad I can taste a whole sheet of aluminum
In my mouth, so I swallow hard,
But I'm so high, I can't concentrate.
He's right, ain't got nothing in my head
And I can't think straight
And can't think about knocking him out cold
And at the same time about consequences.

He's right: he ain't my mother,
But neither is my mother,
Who turned me over to the cops
Like a Judas,
A traitor
To her
Own
Son,
And if she ain't my mother,
Then who am I?
Maybe they're all right:
I may be nothing?

Then here's the note Mr. Ramirez wrote on the bottom of my poem: "Arturo, amazing poem! Conversational, like spoken word. I like the paradox of being and not being. I like the biblical allusion. Whatever you are or aren't, you have the potential to become a poet." I don't know half the stuff he wrote, but me, a poet? Ha. What a joker this Mr. Ramirez is.

If I had to write another poem, it wouldn't be so much like this one, though. I just noticed it's a bit angrier-sounding than my autobiography, but I've had time to settle down a bit, think things through. It'd be a totally different poem.

And thinking about it, maybe I should scrap this story and start over. Try to get it all right next time.

Maybe some action, a real ending besides me still sitting here at the Center trying to do everything they tell me so I won't end up at the Camps. Mr. Ramirez says if I look hard enough I'll find other things to write about. I can toss this in the trash easy and try to go for an exciting story, another story from another time. But my hand is hurting from writing so long already. I'll just stick to this one and hope Mr. Ramirez likes it enough for even a B. It's a true story, and it's about me.

# 7

# MY SELF MYSELF

They're punks—the both of them, always hugging him cozy and patting his back like when he actually was a baby, and whispering in his ear, "Ooh, poor baby, poor thing, are you okay, did she hurt you?"

"I didn't do anything. He did it to himself. Ask him: I didn't even touch the big crybaby," I say to them. I'm on the old, creaky swing set in our backyard. They're sitting on the patio.

My poor excuse for a mother glares at me. My father shakes his head. They think they're doing right by him, but here he is, middle-school age and they treat him like a baby. He'll be a sissyboy if they keep that up.

My way, he'll know what's what in this world and how to deal with it.

"Hush up, Missy!" my mother says. "You hush up. You've done enough harm already. Just shut it."

You shut it, Mabel, I think, but I don't say it. I know if I do Mabel'll let go of Deuce (that's what my dad calls my brother, not Leonard Junior for being named the same). Then she'll jump up and snag me off the swings; so instead I just think it and keep swinging. She won't hold me in her arms. Dad sometimes does, but not in a good long while. So I've learned my own way. Who needs hugs anyway?

What a baby Dewey is. That's what I call him, and he used to cry about it to Mom and Dad—"Missy's not calling me by my right name, Mommy." So I'd get a good talking-to, Mom sometimes shaking me by the arm and saying, "How can you not get it through your thick skull? Be nice to him. Stop teasing. He's only a boy." So, after our "talk" I'd go back to calling him Deuce, but within a week I'd forget the talking-to and the shaking by the arms and call him Dewey. He'd cry again, and again my parents would call me to their room.

You'd think he wasn't in middle school and a starter on the football team, with his constant whimpering. He just now tried getting into Mom's lap, but he's so heavy that even Mom tells him, "Get off me and sit on the floor, baby, you're too big to be sitting on your mommy." But then she rubs his forehead like he likes, and they go inside to watch TV. I stay outside, swinging. The lightning bugs sparkling.

These last couple of weeks he hasn't complained about me calling him Dewey because some of the guys at school, Franky the quarterback for one, also called him Dewey one day at practice. And now the name is cool, and that's supposed to make Dewey cool too because the guys know his name.

Today, right before he went crying to Mabel and Dad, he and I were in the backyard. I was hammering anthills with a croquet mallet, and he was piddling around with his latest invention—a pulley, rigged up to the tree, that's connected to his bedroom window. Dewey's always trying to invent stuff, but his ideas, even though he makes them work, serve zero purpose, I mean none whatsoever. This one seemed it could be good for something, but what kind of a sister would I be, telling him that? Still, I couldn't help looking at it and thinking it would be perfect for sending up secret notes, or food, if he were ever grounded and sent to his room. Like that would ever happen.

This pulley system could only work, though, with two people operating it. One at the bottom pulling on the ropes and the other jailed in my brother's room waiting for the secret goods: a plate of food, a treasure map, or instructions for an escape. So Dewey said to me, "Hey, Missy, come here, will you? Let's see if this works. Come on."

I dropped the mallet and walked over.

"Okay," he said, "I'm gonna go upstairs, and when I say the word, you start pulling."

"What are you going to do?"

"I said, I'm going upstairs, and wait."

"Why don't I go upstairs, and you stay down here and do all the work?"

"It's not work. It's a pulley, duh. It keeps you from having to work. You would think you'd like a tool like this, that lets you be all lazy like you are." He laughed.

When he wanted to, he could be a cool kid, like just then, making a crack like he did, but mostly he whimpered. I had my work cut out.

"Sure, whatever, jerk."

He started for the sliding door, then I asked, "You want me to pull on it this way?" And I pulled on it.

He ran toward me. "No no no. The other way, stupid. Like this." You see, a few months ago, he wouldn't've dared call me stupid. Now it's part of his daily "insult my sister" vocabulary.

I must have jammed the pulley somehow because it wasn't working now that Dewey was pulling on it hard. "You broke it," he said, then I heard a snap, looked up, the pulley came loose, and bonked Dewey on the shoulder.

He looked at me, then grabbed his shoulder, and I said, "You'll be okay. It was only a bump. You're not going to be a sissy and go crying to Mabel, are you?"

Then he screamed out and started crying. That's when my parents came out to the patio, hugged on him, and said, "Ooh, poor baby."

When Dewey settled down, they went in and turned on the TV.

I'm on the swing now, and I can hear the phony TV people talking, that's how loud my family likes it. Through the window at the kitchen and the sliding door I see the light of the TV shining on and off.

For the past two weeks, since Dewey went from being a nobody to a somebody because now he's okay with the name Dewey, I've been trying to come up with another name for him that'll bother him like before. But nothing. Earlier he gave me an idea, though. Right before he got hit with the pulley.

In French class, first thing we learned was the numbers: in French, two is deux, pronounced "dew," or even "doo," as in "doo-doo," but other people might misunderstand and think I'm calling him Dew and say, "What a nice thing to call your brother. You must really like him." But I don't; okay, I do, but so what?

I've got a better idea. He'd said, "It's a pulley, duh!" So that's it: Duh.

The sliding door opens, and there he is. "Hey, Sis, Mom and Dad want you to come inside."

"Hey, you know, in French the number two is pronounced 'dew,' but we're not in France, we're in Georgia, which means we're rednecks. I was going to call you Dew, but it just doesn't sound right, being redneck and all, so I'm gonna call you Duh instead."

He thinks about it for a moment, and I can't see the lights coming on in his head like people say they can see, just a blank stare. Then, "Maw, Missy's calling me names again."

"Grow up," I tell him.

He leaves the door open, and then I hear it. Mabel's screaming for me to come inside.

Then I say, "But I'm just putting to good use all the stuff I'm learning at school. You should be proud of me like you are of Duh when he invents one of his good-for-nothing contraptions and says he learned it in science class."

"I'll have none of that." Like always, she shakes me by the arm and tells me, "Deuce is young and impressionable. He's at a stage in his life where he could go good or bad depending on all kinds of stuff. I don't even want to think of him doing drugs, failing class, or quitting school. Listen, Missy, you're the grown-up here. You can take care of yourself. Your brother's still, you know, so can you help us out a bit?"

Duh doesn't look at me like he used to when he was little, smiling because I was getting in trouble. He stares at the TV instead, then walks out of the room to the kitchen.

"But, Mom," I say.

"No buts, young lady. Apologize to your brother and go up to your room," she says.

And I scream, "I'm sorry for everything, Deuce," then go to my room.

I'll call him that, but when the shaking wears off it'll be back to Duh. I close the door behind me. I lie down on the bed and wonder, looking up at my blank ceiling, Who's worried about what path *I* take? What about *my* self-esteem?

I'll worry about my self myself.

There's a knock at the door. It's Duh, and he says, "Hey, sorry about that. Duh's good, from the pulley comment, right? But I'm getting older now and how do you think it looks a guy being poked fun at by his sister, so would you mind it too much going back to Dewey? I'll stop telling on you." He stands at the door, holding the knob, biting his bottom lip. "So?" he says.

I make like I'm thinking. But it's already been decided. I think all my bugging's finally paid off. "Don't stop whining on my account. Do it for yourself, because I'll tell you what makes you look even stupider than I can is you crying on Momma's shoulder for any and every little thing. What you think those boys on the team would think if they knew that side of you?"

"Yeah, that's cool."

"Then it's settled, Dewey."

He gives me a lopsided smile, cuts the light, then shuts the door, and I'm looking up at the little glow-in-the-dark stars and moon on my ceiling. To see them, I can't look right at them, but sideways. Kind of like how I saw Dewey just now, saw him insignificant and little when looking right at him, and then the next minute all big and bright on a sidewise glance.

There's stars on my ceiling, and I can't stop looking. It's an entire universe up there.

# 8

# UN FAITE

Kiko was sitting by himself today, eating his lunch. Biding his time. Staying out of trouble. He had it all figured out about reinventing himself. Right after he finished middle school in June, his family would be moving to Mission. After summer vacation he'd be starting at a new school in a new town. There, he could become anyone he wanted to be: the serious, silent type, a girl magnet, a bookworm. Anybody but the going-nowhere-fast joker he was right now.

He'd already ruined his reputation in La Joya. Just last week, for example, he almost got the tar beat out of him for having done something he thought was right.

Rumor had it there was going to be a fight between the Soul Survivors, a gang led by Trompo, one of Kiko's cousins, and the mochos, a bunch of Mexicans, del otro lado. Everybody wanting their part of the campus all to themselves and ready to fight for it. At Nellie Schunior

Middle School, these were the two big groups looking for control.

It was supposed to be a good fight since usually the mochos were older because of their language "barrier." Their English sounded all cut up to bits and so the name, mochos. No matter how old, they had to go through the Texas Bilingual Ed program, which put them a year or two behind.

The cholos were hard-core and wore baggy pants, usually cuffed at the ankle, and pressed nice and proper, so trucha that the crease from the waist to the cuffs could almost cut someone. Their shirts were red or blue plaid Pendletons, buttoned only at the collar, over white muscle shirts like Kiko's grandfathers wore. But their glory was their charoles, or Stacies—the shiniest Stacy Adams dress shoes around, and the more soles tacked on, the better to kick with.

Cholos slouched but without looking sloppy. They walked around the school low and slow and in small groups so as not to attract too much attention. Sometimes they took a cruise around the campus with their girlfriends, rucas with long, straight black or brown hair and lots of makeup. Thick and colorful around the eyes. These guys were known as the school's ruffians, always in trouble, always looking for more. Kiko was a cholo.

Kiko belonged to the Soul Survivors, but he didn't want anything to do with any fight. I'll be out of all this when I move, he thought. If I can just make it through this last month of school.

Over lunch today, he was thinking back to last Tuesday, the day of the fight. He had just begun going around with a seventh grader named Janie, one of the school's only blondies, and had dropped her off at her class upstairs. Right as he was turning to leave, he heard a commotion.

He glanced back over his shoulder and that's when all the borlote got started. It began with curses and taunts, turned into heavy breathing, then shoes scuffling on recently waxed floors, and bodies thrown up against and bouncing off lockers, then it was a hurricane of arms and legs flailing.

Eventually Kiko ended up pushed against the lockers, and right in front of him, Trompo was being pounced on by two of the mochos. One of them had his back to Kiko, so Kiko shoved his arm between the mocho's left arm and his ribs. Kiko was somehow able to pull him away from Trompo, who stomped on the other one.

Kiko's guy looked over his shoulder and said, "¿Que onda?" Just then the teachers came and broke up the ruckus. Trompo and a few others got away. Kiko's heart was beating hard, so he paid the mocho no attention because all he'd done was try to keep it even for everybody. Who ever heard of fighting two on one? He hadn't thrown any punches of his own. He hadn't jumped the mocho from behind.

Wednesday, Kiko was walking around the school during lunchtime with Janie. "That was so cool of you, how you handled that guy," she said.

Kiko had to turn his face away so she couldn't see him smiling big.

Out of the corner of his eye Kiko had noticed a group of mochos following them. It was that or they were just out strolling like he and Janie were. He turned to look at them, and then knew he was in trouble when the guys kept walking behind him and Janie not even talking, just looking straight ahead. Kiko knew in his gut that they were looking ahead in time, waiting for a perfect place where they could jump him.

He didn't tell Janie what he was thinking. "Oh, that was nothing," he told her. "Trompo would've done the same for me."

Janie said, "Cool."

Kiko tried focusing on the situation, these guys following him. No, he tried thinking about next year, a new start for him, a clean slate, like his counselor had said last time he was called into the office. He could have that clean slate, but if he got into it with these mochos, then his reputation would follow him. He thought, Solve this, quick. If I stand up to them, I'll get the beating of my life. If that happens, how can I save face with Janie?

That was one of the most important rules for Kiko: under any circumstances, impress your ruca. No matter he was planning on breaking up with her the last day of school. So who cares what she thinks, right? She's not coming with me next year.

If I can just get past the library, over to the science

wing before they jump me, he thought, then I'll be okay. Trompo and the rest of them will be standing either by the gym or by the fire escape, so if I can just make it there, they'll see what's up, and things'll go good.

When he and Janie reached the library he noticed Ramon and his girlfriend sitting on the benches that lined the science wing. He headed right for Ramon, another Soul Survivor.

Kiko told Janie, "I need to tell him something." Ramon walked up and the two girls sat together. The mochos stopped by the library and leaned against the wall.

"Oyes, Kiko," said Ramon. "Have you noticed ese bonche de mochos following you?"

"Siroles, vato," said Kiko. "What do you think?"

"Mira, vato, just walk toward the gym. That's where Trompo is. I'll go tell him we're coming."

"Orale," Kiko said.

"For now, just act normal. Keep walking around with your ruca."

Kiko went back to Janie, who asked him, "Hey, what's going on here?"

"I don't know what you mean," he told her. "But whatever happens, when it happens, take off. Don't stick around. I don't want my girlfriend getting hurt or in trouble because of me."

"What a tough guy. Pues, let's go. And my friends have to ask why I love you."

Kiko didn't want to think about that. Not love. Especially since if things went the way he wanted, she'd soon be part of his past too.

The mochos caught up to Kiko and Janie and walked on by. Kiko thought, Whew, Maybe Ramon and I got it all wrong. Maybe these guys were just walking around. They must've just wanted to scare me. Then Kiko noticed that once he and Janie'd been overtaken, the group of guys had slowed down, then stopped, and turned, and begun to walk toward him in a semicircle.

"Take off," he said to Janie. "I'll see you after math."

"No, but—"

"Do what I say."

Kiko knew he'd be okay because just behind the mochos, leaning up against the wall of the gym, were Trompo, Ramon, and the other vatos who would stand by him through anything. He caught their eye and nodded in their direction.

Trompo nodded back.

"¿Que onda traes tu con nosotros?" asked the biggest of the mochos.

"I don't have a problem with any of you," answered Kiko, mustering all his courage.

"Porque si te quieres meter en lo que no te importa, te damos una friegisa ahorita mismo," said another. Kiko saw it was the mocho he'd pulled off Trompo.

Well, Kiko didn't want to get a pounding from them now or ever. He looked over at his own boys. They had not moved an inch in his direction.

"No hay pedo, vatos," Kiko told them. "It was all a

mistake what I did yesterday, and I don't want no problems with you."

Trompo and the rest were still stuck to the gym wall.

"Nadamas fijate donde metes tu nariz, o te la quebramos," warned the big one.

Kiko liked his nose right where it was just fine, so he apologized for having stuck it in other people's business. "No hay pedo conmigo."

They gave him a good long stare and finally turned and walked away. Once they were gone, the Soul Survivors walked in his direction.

"Oyes, Kiko, ¿que querian esos mochos?" asked Trompo.

"Yeah, why did they leave all of a sudden?" said Pablito. "We were ready, vato. Listos para ponerles una chingisa."

"Nada. They didn't want nothing," Kiko answered.

"But Ramon said—"

"They didn't want nothing," Kiko repeated, and walked away.

"Let him go," Trompo said. "Kiko, I knew you could take care of yourself, and I was thinking ahead. I want to be around to fight another day. This wasn't the time. I'm planning something bigger."

"Orale, no hay pedo," said Kiko.

Janie was waiting for him at the side door to the school. In his mind he knew: I did the right thing yesterday, getting involved in the fight like I did. Today, the mochos had been wrong to jump him. But worse, his own cousin didn't come help him out like Kiko'd done for him.

Janie took his arm and wrapped it over her shoulders. "Well," she said, "you can get them later."

"Yeah, later," he said.

That was last week. Today, walking to dump his lunch tray, he knew what he needed to do. He wouldn't make any waves before the end of the school year. He'd play it cool and smooth with Janie. And when it was time, he'd tell her, "I'm taking off for Mission, baby, and I don't want to hold you back." She'd maybe cry, maybe not. Maybe she'd be ready for a change too. To Trompo he'd say, "Orale, primo, I got your back if you ever come out to Mission." He'd secretly hope Trompo wouldn't ever visit.

Truth was, he didn't want any connection to this place, to this time. Maybe there, in Mission, he thought, I'll get all new clothes, read a couple books, be regular. No more of this Soul Survivor business. No more fighting. Just be an average Joe.

Kiko couldn't help smiling. He'd figured it out. Now he couldn't wait. He thought he'd go see the librarian, get a list of books he should read over the summer. He knew the others couldn't see it, but inside he felt he had already begun to change.

# 9

# MANNY CALLS

Manny knew full well he wasn't talking to his grandfather every weekend when he dialed the old man up.

His grandfather'd died two years before from a second heart attack, and another operation would've not helped but hurt more since the heat down in Texas was so heavy on the old man's chest after the first operation, so why bother with it? He'd sat around breathing hard, like swallowing a bucket of water. He'd gotten better, though, even going back to the Cultural Center for Older Adults and taking up square dancing. Soon after, Manny had taken off to college out of state. Then his grandfather had died several months later.

Manny understood it was a recording that answered every time he dialed up his grandfather: This number has been disconnected, if you'd like to try again, etc., and then the beepbeepbeep—over and over until Manny was done talking. Making like he was really talking to his grandfather was his way of letting go of stuff: talk his way through all kinds of problems; sometimes just talk; or tell jokes he'd heard that week. Like the one about the boy whose dad sends him to a Catholic school because he's failing miserably in his math class, and no matter the threats and bribes from the dad, the boy still does poorly, so up to the nuns he goes, and after a week at the Catholic school with the nuns the boy shows incredible improvement and keeps getting better grades as the weeks pass and the dad can't believe it and so the dad asks, How? and the boy says, All it took me was to see that guy nailed to that plus sign up at the front of the church and I knew I had to do better or else. Manny knew his grandfather, had he heard that joke, being the religious man he had been, maybe most likely wouldn't have laughed, more likely shaken his head instead and walked away from Manny because he'd just made fun of Jesus. But when he called he'd tell it anyway. It was a machine he'd be telling it to and not his grandfather. Manny knew that.

When he was done talking, shaking his head yes or no, or slapping his knee and laughing because if his grandfather'd still been alive, he would tell some jokes while doling out advice, when Manny was done talking, he'd sit and think about the old days, hanging out at his grandfather's, drinking tea. And he'd tell his grandfather, It was so funny how back then you'd pull out your teeth and soak them in the tea.

They'd laugh, then Manny'd hang up and go about his business.

When his grandfather died, Manny couldn't afford a bus ticket home for the funeral. He had just barely enough to keep his one-bedroom place another month or so and eat Hamburger Helper the whole time, plus what he could sneak from the restaurant. His place was beyond the highway, up a stretch from the school but within walking distance, or a bike ride on days he was running late. It had ugly green walls. Like avocado dip.

On the night he found out his grandfather had died, he'd been working at the restaurant at the fryers. He got a call from Penelope, the girl he was kind of dating. She came over three or four nights out of the week. He'd get in after work and there she was, at the kitchen table doing homework, or watching TV, waiting up for him. She always jotted down his phone messages and taped them up to the fridge. That night she called at work and told him, Your grandpa's taken ill, another heart attack, and it doesn't look good for him, hon. He hung up and went back to the fryers, quiet the whole rest of the night, dropping fries, wings, and chicken fingers. He thought about the time they'd gone to clean his grandmother's plot at the cemetery. His grandfather on his knees, pulling out the weeds and brushing clean the headstone, rubbing real gentle over her name. The old man had said, Won't be long and I'll be here, next to her. Then Manny said, No ways, Pop. You'll live longer than the moon.

When it got near closing time and only the bar regulars were still hanging around, he asked, Can I leave early to call home?

Why's that? the manager asked.

He said, My grandfather's ill and I need to find out how he is.

The manager said, Okay, we've got a good closing crew tonight. We should be all right. Just shut down all but one fryer, will you?

When he got to his apartment, smelling of grease like always, Penelope was gone. Manny was thinking she was *gone* gone, because you'd think on a night like tonight with your grandfather close to dying that your girl'd be there to comfort you. Who does she think she is! he said, and balled up both fists, and shook in the dark hallway.

Later he found out that she'd only left for a few moments to go buy some ice cream for him and on the way back there'd been a wreck, and the emergency guys took forever to clean up the mess.

But when he got home he cursed at her for abandoning him, then tried calling home. He couldn't get hold of anybody until late, and his dad said, Here's the number to the hospital. Ask for the ICU waiting room, that's where your mother is, but son, your grandfather's already died. About an hour ago. Son . . . yeah, so you better call your mom.

Manny hung up and cried, sitting in his tore-up brown leather chair. He punched at the armrests. Then he got it together and called the number his dad had given him, but it was the wrong number. He called home again, but there was no answer now. He couldn't reach Penelope, either, so he hit the sack. He fell asleep thinking he kept hearing his grandfather calling him from the kitchen. Once he got up, but it was nothing.

The ice cream had melted all the way through when Penelope got home, and she woke him and they slurped up a bowl each, her hand on his knee, the whole time patting it.

The following day he spoke to his mom. She was quiet a moment, then said, I feel so alone without him. She told Manny about the days leading up to his death. How for a couple nights before he had stayed up with her, late, and talked all night long, not a single complaint the whole time. Just the old days and his gardens. The next day, the heaviness in his chest came back, so she went over to his place for the evening, and he took his medicines and was okay to sleep, but halfway through the night, she woke up and found him gone from his room. He was sitting at the kitchen table, praying, and he said, No, but you talk to me, when she had asked him if he wanted to talk some. Then he said his tongue was going numb, and she called the aunts and uncle, and the ambulance took him to the hospital, where he went into a coma and never woke up.

She cried and Manny felt bad because he was also the only one not going to the funeral, except for one of his cousins living somewhere in Germany. And his mom said, That's okay. If you don't have the money what can you do? But I'd really love to see you. She stayed quiet a bit longer and so did Manny, then they said goodbye and hung up. That was two years ago.

Tonight, Manny wanted to study for his Calc II test tomorrow. He'd called over to Daniela's house and talked his way out of their regular Wednesday-night date at the bowling alley. He and Penelope had broken up a long time ago.

He opened up his book and notebook and started reading over his notes and looking over some of his homework. Then he picked up the phone and dialed his grandfather. He wanted to tell him about his test, how he would probably score the highest grade on this exam of all the students. Eventually finish in the top ten percent of his class. He took a deep breath to start talking: Grandfather, he said.

Then, Hello? Who's this? a girl asked. Who do you want to talk with? Ain't no grandfather at this number. Hello? You got the wrong number. Then, to someone else grumbling in the background: Shhh, shhh. Just a wrong number. Some guy wanting to talk to his grand-daddy. Go back to sleep, and she hung up.

Manny hung up too. It was close to midnight back in Texas, one A.M. here. Manny was surprised the phone company hadn't reassigned his grandfather's number sooner. Even so, expecting it to sometime happen didn't make it easier now to hear a stranger's voice and not a recording's or his grandfather's.

He sat on his leather chair and stared at the keypad on his phone. It was still lit up. A few seconds passed and the numbers shut off. He kept staring, though: What do I do? What do I do? chewing at the soft insides of his mouth. Out of habit, without thinking, Manny ran his thumb over the numbers, not actually dialing, just rubbing at the pads. He couldn't be sure: maybe he'd smashed a five instead of an eight. But what if he called and got that strange woman again? But if he didn't try, he wouldn't know. He could wait till morning, but then he wouldn't have slept at all thinking it over, and worse, not gotten in any serious study time for his exam tomorrow.

So he dialed, calling out the numbers as he pressed them to make sure, and again, Who's this? Don't you know what time it is and people have to work tomorrow and here you are calling at all hours?

Sorry, I got the wrong number.

Damn straight! and she hung up hard.

He got up and replaced the phone on the cradle. He walked back to the kitchen table and opened up his textbook and his notebook, twirled his pen a few moments, then started writing a letter.

When he was done with it, he looked for an envelope. He had to go into his closet where he kept all kinds of boxes full of papers and old bills. He found an envelope that had been written on: Receipts; but he crossed that out and wrote in his grandfather's name and address and put a stamp on. No return address. He walked down to the box on the corner and dropped the letter in.

"Look at them, Papi," said Melly to her father.

Mr. Otero cast his line into the water again and looked up and to his right. "Tan locos, mi'ja. It's a crazy thing to do."

From upriver, Melly and her father could see five or six boys fixing to jump from Jensen's Bridge. They pounded their chests, inched their way to the edge, then dove in all at once, some headfirst, others feet first, and one balled up. The boys disappeared underwater, leaving behind them different-sized splashes, then Melly heard the echoes of their jumping screams a full second or two after they'd gone under. By then, they were shooting up out of the water, their arms raised in the air. They'd done it. Most of the boys in Three Oaks had to dive from the bridge at one time or other to prove themselves real men. Today was their day.

Melly saw the boys crawl from the river and turn

over on their backs, stretched out like lizards sunning themselves on the bank. Reeling in her line, she thought, So what if they can dive off the bridge! I could do it too if I wanted. Who said it was just for the guys to do?

"You'll do nothing of the kind," said Mr. Otero.

"Huh?"

"You said you could dive too if you wanted?"

"I didn't say anything. You must be hearing things."

He smiled. "Just like your mother. Talking your thoughts aloud." He reached over and touched his rough hand to her cheek.

Melly blushed. She stood and set her rod on a rock, then stretched. She held her face and wondered if it was red from the sun. Red from her father's touch?

All along she'd actually been talking. She'd heard the same thing from her tías, from Mamá Tochi, and from her sister, Becky. "Your mom literally spoke her mind," the aunts all told her.

"You're so much like your mother," Mr. Otero told her, casting again.

"She probably would've jumped," she said.

"Probably so, but I said you won't do it. ¿M'entiendes?"

"Yes, sir. I understand. No jumping from the bridge." She looked downriver, then set her sight on the bridge. Her face was warm, and she imagined her mother jumping from the bridge, her long black hair in a ponytail, or all loose and curly; her mother slicing into the water, then exploding out, all smiles and laughter. Beautiful.

"What?"

"What what?"

"Never mind. Just like your mother."

That evening, Melly went to visit her grandmother, Mamá Tochi, down the street from where Melly lived with her father and her sister, who'd only recently left for college.

Mamá Tochi had lived on her own ever since Melly's grandfather died five years ago. When Mamá Tochi's children all moved and married, each begged her to come live with them, but she refused. She said, "For decades I took care of both your father and myself when you left the house for work and school, and before that I took care of the six of you, from dirty diapers to broken hearts, so what makes you think I need to be looked after?"

Mr. Otero, Melly's dad, was the only one to pull up stakes and move to be closer to Mamá Tochi when Papá 'Tero died. Moving was easy for him. His own wife had died a year before his father's passing, and he once confessed to Mamá Tochi, "With Aurelia gone, I don't know that I can do right by our two girls."

Melly knocked at her grandmother's and walked in. It was early evening, so she knew that Mamá Tochi would be out in her backyard garden with her babies: the herbs that ran up along the house; then the rosales, four bushes of them, red, yellow, white, and pink, big as trees almost; countless wildflower patches; and Melly's favorite, the esperanza bushes, the yellow bells soft on her cheeks. The backyard smelled like honey tasted.

She went out the screen door and said, "Mamá Tochi. Where are you?" Melly could hear the water splashing, but couldn't quite make out her grandmother.

"Aqui, mi'jita. I'm over here." Mamá Tochi was hidden behind the esperanza bush, watering it with her pail. She'd set the hose at the base of one of the rosales. "You don't even have to tell me why you're here. You want to jump from that crazy bridge."

Sometimes Melly thought her grandmother could read minds, see into the future, even talk to the dead. Melly couldn't figure out why she came over for advice. She never got anything but cuentos from Mamá Tochi, stories that somehow served as life lessons. That time Melly had had the chance to cheat on her end-of-term exam her ninth-grade year, Mamá Tochi said, "I remember a time I was calling bingo. Playing that night was my worst enemy, Perla. I kept an eye all night on her four cards, praying a secret prayer that she'd lose every time. On one of her cards I could see all she needed was El Gallo. Without knowing why, I pulled a card from the middle of the deck instead of the top. I pulled La Chalupa, and Manuela won. I was afraid to even look at the top card. I collected all the others and shuffled them real fast. What if it had been El Gallo? I wasn't able to look in Perla's eyes for two weeks and a half, that's how guilty I felt."

Lessons to be learned that time? You do it, you'll get caught. You'll feel worse if you don't get caught.

"It won't be cheating, really, Mamá Tochi. The teacher's already said chances of me passing are slim. There's stuff on the test we've never studied even."

Mamá Tochi sat on the porch swing and said, "You're a big girl. You'll know what to do."

That night, Melly considered what her grandmother had said. She saw herself three years later, marching for graduation, everyone taking photos, everyone smiling, everyone happy, except she wouldn't be because she'd remember having cheated that time back in the ninth grade. She didn't sleep at all that night. The next day, even before the exam was handed out, two boys and one girl were called out of class. Earlier in the week, they had asked Melly if she wanted a look at the test. They'd found it in one of the teacher's desks and ran off a copy. The morning of the test, she told them, "No thanks. I'll just try my best. I'll fail on my own terms, you know." Then they got busted, and Melly passed the test by two points. "A pass is a pass," said Mamá Tochi. That's just what Melly's mom used to say.

Tonight, Melly said, "What d'you mean? I'm here to visit with my favorite Mamá Tochi."

"Don't give me that. Your papi's already called. He's worried you're gonna jump and get tangled up in the weeds at the bottom of the river and drown."

Melly said, "Ah, Papi knows there's no weeds down there. And besides, no one's ever drowned at the bridge before."

Mamá Tochi put down the pail, turned off the hose, then said, "Sit down. I'll bring coffee."

Melly sat under the orange tree. Papá 'Tero had built the table and chairs years ago. He also had carved each of his children's and grandchildren's names and dates of birth into the tabletop in a great big circle. At the center were his name and Mamá Tochi's: Servando Otero and Rosario Garcia de Otero, their dates of birth, and the date of their wedding. Melly traced Mamá Tochi's name.

"I put two spoons of sugar and a little milk in yours, just like you drink it," said Mamá Tochi.

"Gracias," said Melly. "It's not that high of a jump— ten, fifteen feet at most."

"That's not high. About two of my rosebushes, right." Mamá Tochi looked up where the top of the invisible bush would be.

"I mean, if the guys can do it— Aren't you the one always saying, 'You can do anything and everything you set your heart to'?"

"You're right, mi'jita. Anything is possible. How's your coffee?"

"Good, thank you, Mamá Tochi."

"Mi'jita, have I ever told you that my mother never let me drink coffee? It was a grown-up thing to do. I didn't take my first drink of it until I was twenty-one."

Melly knew there was a reason Mamá Tochi was telling her this. She just had to figure it out. She had to pay attention, then sleep on it, and if she hadn't figured it out by after school tomorrow, she'd have to come visit a second time, get another story, then try to figure out two lessons instead of one.

"I'd gotten my first job as a seamstress," Mamá Tochi continued. "My first paycheck, I told my mother, 'First thing I'll buy is a cup of coffee at Martin's Café.' My mother said, 'Then you'll buy for us all.' And so I did, a cup of coffee and a piece of sweet bread for everyone, all thirteen of us, I spent every peso I'd made, and I didn't sleep all night. But I loved the taste so much I haven't stopped, even when Dr. Neely told me I should. What does he know?"

She sat across the table from Melly and sipped her coffee.

Melly thought she'd figured out the lesson: that she should dive, and then she wouldn't be able to stop. She'd be as old as Mamá Tochi and diving would still be in her blood, and one day she'd jump from a bridge too high for such a frail woman and break every bone in her body and drown. But she'd be doing what she loved.

"This is some good coffee," Mamá Tochi said.

"Sure is. Good bread, too."

"Twenty-one, can you believe it? Today you kids have all these fancy cafés in your fancy bookstores where you go and study with all your friends. What was that drink you bought me once? Iced café mocha? Why ruin a good cup of coffee with chocolate syrup? Why ruin it by pouring it into a paper cup? Not like in the old days. A little crema, a pinch of sugar, and steaming hot in a clay jar."

It only seemed like Mamá Tochi had finished telling her story. Melly knew better, so she leaned back, ready for more. She knew she hadn't figured out her grandmother's riddle yet.

"Nowadays, you babies grow up too fast. You're women before you're girls. You never get to be girls, some of you. It's not a bad thing, the way the world is today. You have to know more sooner, and be able to survive it. In my day, all I had to worry about was drinking my first cup of coffee, my first job, and hoping my family would choose the right man for me. They did that back then, you know, chose your husband. My father tried to find the man for me, and—well, let's just say, I was ahead of my time when I told my father I would not marry Marcos Antonio Velasquez. Papá told me, '¿Y tu, quien te crées?' I was twenty-three then, and getting too old to be playing this game, my father said. But I—I had to take a stand sometime. After all," she said, and laughed. Melly imagined Mamá Tochi's young face laughing, her wrinkles somehow gone. "After all, I was a woman now. I was drinking coffee at Martin's every Friday afternoon on my way home. But I didn't smoke like some of the others. I tried that once, but once was all I needed. I didn't like the taste.

Coffee, now there's taste. Tobacco? Take it or leave it. Better leave it." She sipped some more, then said, "Mi'jita, it's getting late. You better go home before your papi calls looking for you."

Melly stood and helped her with the cups and plate of bread. She hooked the screen door shut. She didn't close the inside door. Mamá Tochi always said she wanted to smell her flowers. "And what's there in this house to steal? I wish someone would come and take that television. It's just something else I have to dust." Melly knew Mamá Tochi was teasing. She liked to watch her Mexican soaps.

"Dive if you want, mi'jita. I know you can make it. You won't drown. You're strong like all those boys, and smarter. So if you feel you have to, then go ahead, jump from that bridge. It'll make you feel better."

Melly hugged her grandmother tight, then said, "Buenas noches, Mamá Tochi."

"Buenas."

Melly was happy. She'd gotten her grandmother's permission. Now her father couldn't say anything about it.

Melly woke to someone revving a car engine down the street. She'd gone to sleep thinking about her grandmother standing up to her own father, looking him in the eye: "I will not marry that boy. I don't love him." Melly imagined her great-grandfather stomping his foot, crinkling his face, pointing at his daughter, and not able to say a word to her. That's how angry Melly imagined him to be, so angry he was speechless. Then later, as the young Mamá Tochi was falling asleep, Melly pictured her great-grandfather bursting into the bedroom to say, "No daughter of mine— I shouldn't have let you drink coffee." And that would be it. He'd slam the door shut, and Rosario wouldn't have to marry Marcos Antonio Velasquez.

Instead she married Servando Otero, a handsome man till the end of his days. Melly remembered how his unshaven face had scratched at her cheeks when he held her tight to him. Like her own father's face tickled her cheeks now when he didn't shave on weekends. Earlier, at the river, she had noticed more gray in her father's stubble. She'd reached over and rubbed his face. He'd touched her cheek. She laughed and said, "I hope my face isn't as hard as yours."

He shook his head. "Not in a million years. You're face is like your mom's. Soft. Very much a woman's face."

Melly caressed her cheek. Like mom, she thought.

"Yep, so much like her. Don't get me wrong. You're hard as nails inside. Tough, and thick-headed, too." He cast his rod again and said, "Just like your mom."

That's when she saw the boys jumping.

In bed, she felt her cheek where her father had touched it. She knew she wouldn't jump. She didn't have to. She was already grown. Had a woman's face. Had nothing to prove to anybody. Tomorrow, if she wanted to, she could tell her father, "I'm diving no matter what you say." But she wouldn't. She was already drinking coffee, like her Mamá Tochi.

Melly turned onto her side. The window was open, and a cool breeze blew in. Melly could smell the sweetness of the flowers and herbs wafting from across the street. She smiled, closed her eyes, and slept.

## I

The day Danny De Los Santos was found by accident, he'd been dead a long time. His body was "severely decomposed," one reporter said, "beyond recognition," said another. That was scary to me because I couldn't help thinking of a dead kitten I found once in our backyard. His stomach was bloated and his little lips were pulled back so his tiny teeth were showing, almost like he was smiling wicked, devilish. I could still tell he was a kitten, though. I remembered how Danny had looked sitting under the tree in front of Americo Paredes Middle School band hall, writing in his journal, leaning back on the tree, his knees pulled up to support his notebook. His hair combed tight. The kitten kept creeping into my mind whenever I tried to imagine Danny under the tree.

I sat in front of the television with my father and mother, listening to the reporter going over the news I'd seen earlier on the set at Pete's house. I couldn't tell exactly where she was, but when the cameraman panned around I could see what looked like Expressway 83 off in the distance. Expressway 83 was within sight of my front yard. All I had to do was stand over by the tree and look right, and there it was, cars passing by with their windows rolled up, going somewhere.

I closed my eyes instead of watching the news and tried to look up and down the expressway in my mind, trying to figure out where this reporter was. I could make out the stretch of road from Peñitas all the way to Mercedes, and in the other direction all the way to Laredo. I traveled both directions like in a helicopter, but I still didn't know where the woman was reporting from.

"Police, as yet," she said, "have no clues, but want to assure the public that they are putting every available man on the case. Parents should be especially watchful over their children."

My father took a deep breath and held it; my mother was crying: "Ay, pobres de sus padres. Que Diosito los ayude."

I was kind of praying too, but I was thinking more about Danny than about his parents: poor Danny, whose face I can't recall anymore. A few minutes ago I could have made him out in my mind, but not now. I tried to put him under the tree, writing, hair tight, but he wasn't Danny anymore.

My father looked at my mother and held her hand, and let out his breath. "You won't be staying out after dark anymore. Understand?" he said.

"I want to know where you are every moment of the day," said my mother.

There went my summer.

I went to my room, where I couldn't sleep, and all I could say to my dad when he checked in on me later was "Okay."

## II

Earlier that day, before any reporters, I'd been over at Pete's with David and Mando watching *Gilligan's Island,* then came the news flash about the body being found, and David said, "Oh, man, this is too heavy. I'm out of here." So Pete turned off the TV and we sat out on the porch. None of us said a word about the news.

Pete, David, Mando, and I were talking, like always, just talking.

"I can't wait to be in the ninth grade," said Pete. I could see his knee was shaking more than usual, like a little epileptic seizure.

"We'll be big time then, right. Older girls with bodies that just won't quit," said Mando.

Then we were quiet again. I wanted to ask what they were thinking. I didn't know how to. Just throw it out there? "Hey, what do you think about Danny being found dead?" No way. My knee was beginning to shake some. Danny stuck in my chest and then sank back down into my lungs. The county sheriff had said, "The investigation is still under way, so we can't comment on any aspect of the physical details and/or nature of the crime scene."

David said, "This is for the birds," and left the porch to get a drink from the hose.

Mando was lean and tall and had green eyes. Sometimes, like this afternoon on the porch, his green eyes seemed to be working extra hard, staring out into the front yard. What are you looking for? I wanted to ask him. That question stuck in my chest too.

Instead, I said, "Yeah, in high school all the girls are babes." When no one said anything, I added, "No more of that stuff we had to put up with from those little girls in middle school. We'll have our own chances at hooking up with women now." I didn't know what I was saying. I just couldn't take the quiet.

Just then I heard my father's famous whistle, his "it's time to come home, or else" whistle. He must have seen the news.

The sun had begun to set, and I hadn't noticed. My dad would keep up with the whistling until I answered from somewhere down the street where I knew he couldn't see us: "Hay voy!" I yelled. "I'm coming."

Like always, I shook hands with all my pals, who lined up, and each tilted his head back without losing eye contact and said either "Te huacho" or "Nos vemos."

"Yeah, I'll see you tomorrow."

Walking down the road, I noticed that there were more parents than usual out on their front porches, and even out on the edges of their yards keeping an eye out. They'd heard the news too. I wondered, Do they even know what they're looking for?

## III

David's mom was calling for him to get home now. Just like every other mom and dad. Not that she didn't love her David, but since his dad just took off into Mexico one day with another woman, and since David was the oldest son, he was the man of the house and didn't need looking after like the rest of us.

What's worse? I used to think. My dad whistling and embarrassing fire out of me, or her not coming out looking for him? But that afternoon she had come out, and the way she was stretching her neck and peering into the long shadows of the trees, then how she began calling him, stuck in my mind: at first, "David. David," really soft, but like she was crying; and then, "David, David!" more urgent, and I couldn't help thinking that she was afraid he had left her too. Or at least that's how the wind from the north made it sound.

I reached the corner of our yard and saw both my mother and father waiting. This is big, I thought. It's never both of them waiting for me. My mother always came out earlier to call me in for supper and Dad came out much later to collect me.

"You need to be coming home immediately when I call you," my father yelled, and put his hand on my shoulder. "Do you hear?"

"Where have you been, Juan?" my mother asked. "You shouldn't be staying out so late. You worry me so."

"Huh?"

"Don't talk back to your mother, son," my father warned. We went in and watched the rest of the news. Over and over, on every channel, "A boy's life has come to a tragic end."

## IV

"That's just it," I was always saying to the others when my parents would get after me, "we're doing and saying our thing, and parents just don't get it. It's impossible to set them straight, you know. They've forgotten what it's like to be our age; we come from two completely different worlds and the odds of understanding one another are zilch."

But tonight, instead of getting all upset and huffy at my father for screaming, I settled down. I knew my father wasn't angry with me. He even told me, "Your mom and I just get worried. Don't want the same thing to happen to you that—" Then he cleared his throat, and I said, "Okay."

## V
———

That spring, in the weeks before the cops found Danny, when he was just missing, our parents weren't worrying so much over us, so we hung out at the ditch. We were thinking Danny would show up, tattered and hungry, but home again; our parents watched us from behind the rosebushes, or telephoned neighbors to make sure we were where we said we would be. It was okay what they were doing, except that it felt like they were spying on us all the time.

Early on, we hadn't thought anything about Danny's disappearance really. He had plain and simple run away. He fit the mold. At school, Danny De Los Santos was a loner. He had maybe one or two friends he hung out with every once in a while, but preferred to sit alone during lunch under the big tree out in front of the band hall. He was always reading. And thick books too. Books the high school kids were also reading. Books we couldn't find in our rinky-dink library. And he was also always writing in a journal.

Not like the journals our English teachers made us keep that I knew they would read no matter what they said about how these were our own private journals and they wouldn't read them. "Trust me, all I'm doing is counting the number of words," Mr. Salinas always said.

But I knew better—teachers didn't have lives outside of school, Mr. Salinas included, so what we wrote would make for the only excitement in their boring lives. I tried to make mine as juicy as possible. A couple times I even wrote in some curse words, but all I got was a grade at the top of the sheet, and sometimes Mr. Salinas wrote comments like "Good work, Juan!" or "You need to make your entries longer for a better grade."

Except for Pete making fun of me the first time I tried to keep a journal outside of class, I enjoyed writing in it. I always wondered if what I was writing was like what Danny was writing in his. I bet not. I just wrote day-to-day stuff. Sometimes nothing at all. He always looked so concentrated, so focused, he had to have been writing nothing but deep stuff. Feelings and such.

I didn't know how to feel about Danny himself. It seemed he never needed to be around other people. I mean, he was a smart student, independent, but did he ever want to date the prettiest girl and whisper a poem in her ear after a football game? Did he ever want to take part in the weekly food fights in the cafeteria? Or to hang out with guys like us and talk about girls and high school like we did?

## VI

So we decided he was a runaway. "Who could be happy always reading and writing like that?" said Pete. Pete was one of three boys and four girls, plus his extended family: both sets of abuelitos, primos, tíos and tías: all under one roof, and some more cousins in the storage shed his dad converted into an apartment when there was no more room in the house. He was always saying, "There's just no place to stretch out, man. I can't wait to get out of there. Solo. No one but me." He felt he knew what Danny was going through at the time: "He wants to be alone for a while, straighten out in his head whatever's not straight, but he'll be back."

We all agreed. Danny's life must have been rough. He was never in trouble at school, but he was never out of it either. We had heard that his teachers wanted to put him in Special Ed because he was antisocial. The day his father showed up at school was the last time the counselors and teachers mentioned anything about Special Ed. He met with all of them; Gracie, the principal's secretary, told Angela, the copy lady, who told anybody who would listen. "One man, all by himself, y muy humilde el, very soft-spoken, solo against all of Danny's teachers, the counselors con todos sus libros and paperwork on Danny, and Mr. Robledo. I was there taking notes." Apparently, they all talked to Mr. De Los Santos about Danny's lack of social skills. They felt he needed to be tested. "Mr. De Los Santos didn't say anything for a few moments, looked at each person there—even Mr. Robledo turned his eyes—'Well,' he said to them, 'my son knows more than all of you put together. If you want to test him, I dare you to put your scores next to his and see who's smart and who's not.' He said that if they kept on with this nonsense, he'd sue the district, and not for money, but for their jobs, each and every one. He got up and left all of them, staring big-eyed. Ay, Angela, you should have seen it." After that, no more talk of Danny needing to be in special classes.

I knew Danny was like that genius Einstein our English teacher was always telling us about. Mr. Salinas told us how back in Einstein's day, his teachers thought he was dumb because he was always flunking math and babbling stuff his teachers didn't understand. Mr. Salinas said, "It was that his teachers *couldn't* understand. This boy was thinking centuries ahead of all his teachers' abilities combined. What they couldn't understand, they feared; and so they tried keeping him down."

I knew that if people would just look into Danny's journal, they'd find something special there. So what if he was "antisocial"? I mean, unless you were lucky like me, really good friends were hard to come by.

## VII

"Where do you think he ran away to?" asked Mando. He was smoothing the grass of the ditch. "I would go to Hawaii, I think."

"Yeah, Hawaii," repeated Pete. "The babes on the beach. Where would you go, Juan?"

"Me? I don't know. Maybe up to California. I got family there."

"So, let me get this straight, you would be running away from one family to another?" said Pete. "What a doofus."

"Well, I didn't say I'd go to my family. I just said I got family there. It's not the same, buey," I answered. "I've been there when I was little and I remember liking it."

"Whatever, Mexican!" said Pete. He made a "W" by touching the tips of his thumbs together and pointing out his index fingers and then he turned over the "W" to form an "M."

I reached over to him and poked my index and middle fingers into his sternum.

"Orale, vato!" he said. He hated that because it was all bone and nerves there, so it hurt him.

David corralled us back into the conversation about Danny: "You know, I talked to him a couple of times."

I was surprised because David doesn't like making new friends. At parties, he'll sit in a chair in the corner of a room and if somebody talks with him, fine; if not, just as fine. With us it's different. We grew up together, so he's always talking. Some days nonstop. But with others, popular as he is, he's almost quiet like Danny. Except I don't think Danny would ever have gone to one of our parties. Maybe because they were both quiet types was what allowed David to talk to Danny.

"I asked him what book he was reading. He said it was called something like *A Clock Works Orange*. He showed it to me, but I didn't get it. He said it was good because it proved how easy it was to brainwash a person. I told him I didn't like to read so much. I thought he was going to laugh at that, but he didn't. He just shook his head and said, 'Yeah.'"

"What'd he do then?" I asked.

"He closed his book. Then he asked me about football. Just like that. 'How do you like quarterbacking?' he said. I didn't even think he knew about football, much less that I was the quarterback. I told him I liked it all right. I told him I'd see him around. That I didn't want to take up his reading time. 'No problem,' he said. 'See you.' And he went back to reading. That's it."

We sat on the bent buffalo grass and thought about what David had just told us. I don't know what everyone else was thinking. I thought, I wish David would talk to me that way, about books, about football not being the most important thing in his life, anything really. I didn't have an older brother or boy cousins, so he was it for me. And all I could think at that moment was how I wish he would talk to me that way, about deep subjects, or stuff that might be embarrassing, like him not liking to read. He had wanted to find out about Danny, while David and I just talked about regular easy stuff. I hoped Danny wouldn't come back, that he'd run farther and farther away. Not look back.

## VIII

After David told us about talking to Danny, I got my mom to take me to the public library in Mission. I got there and asked the man behind the counter if he knew this book, and he said, "Oh, you mean *A Clockwork Orange*." He looked at me funny, then looked the title up on his computer and said, "It's in, but it might be a bit too risqué for you. How old are you?"

I didn't say anything, just stood there looking at him.

"Wait here," he said, then came back with the book. He ran it through his system and asked me to sign the card.

I took my time, turned it over and back to see if this was the copy Danny had read from. It wasn't.

The old guy said, "It's due in two weeks."

Well, I didn't finish it in two weeks because I was a slow reader, plus I was reading it in secret. And to make it worse, I wasn't understanding much of it, so I had to go back and check it out another two times. I also got up the nerve to ask Mr. Salinas about what was going on in the story with all of the strange words. He said I should use the glossary of terms at the end of the book, and that eventually, I wouldn't have to look at the definitions. "That's one of the beauties of this book," he said, turning it over in his hand, "that you learn without knowing it. Almost like you're being brainwashed." He also told me the basic story line of the book so I wouldn't be completely lost. "If you've got questions about it, just ask," he told me. He patted me on the shoulder and said, "Good to see you improving yourself through literature."

What stuck in my mind was that he had said the

same thing about it as Danny had said to David: people can be brainwashed.

Did Danny and Mr. Salinas discuss this book? Probably not, because Danny didn't have Mr. Salinas for English.

After Danny's body was found, I wondered, had he been part of a brainwashing? Maybe that's how he ended up the way he did?

## IX

"So, if you ran away, where would you go, David?" I asked that day in the ditch. I looked away to the fields. I didn't want to talk about Danny anymore.

"Why go anywhere?" he answered, and left it at that.

We sat there until the sun made the field across from us gold, and then the shadows began creeping up on the rows and rows of dirt ready for the next crop. Eventually, we left and played some football. Meanwhile, our parents, and I mean the whole barrio of them, were out and about, mothers whispering to other mothers, fathers drinking a beer with other fathers at the edges of their yards, and all of them keeping an eye on us. Danny hadn't been missing long, but it was long enough for our parents.

On the news that night, we saw a picture of Danny, a snapshot of him in what could have been his front yard, his journal nestled under his arm. They also showed an interview with Danny's father, whose eyes were raw from crying. He begged parents to spend as much time with their children as possible, to hover over them no matter how much we said we hated it. That it was their duty as parents. "One never knows . . . ," he said, and nothing more. During the interview he didn't cry, though. He was solemn. He was as strong as a father should be.

The reporter said, "If you have any information on this boy's mysterious disappearance, please call this number." A number flashed across the screen.

## X

The serious neighborhood speculating began the second morning after Danny was found. Nobody wanted to pour the bad salt on their own family by speaking publicly on the first day about an innocent boy and how he was killed. It was Saturday, and I was at the Korner Store drinking a root beer.

Old Man Charlie, the grandfather of the only white family in our barrio, was talking to Junior the Clerk. "No'mbre, some people say the boy just run away, ran into some bad luck then. I think different," he said. He sounded like us because all his life he'd spent alongside our abuelos, working in the same fields at the same pay.

"So, what's your idea happened to the boy?" asked Junior the Clerk.

Old Man Charlie hardly ever left his chair on his porch. But today he'd come out. He must have been thinking about this all night. "I think he was kidnapped. The boy was taken by force. I don't know what for, but there's all sorts of bad folks in this world. You never know what somebody would want to do to a boy, but they're out there." He lit his third cigarette and swallowed the smoke like sucking down a Coca-Cola. He coughed and released only a part of what he had taken in. It wasn't but two years earlier that Charlie was forced to stay on his front porch, scars from his surgery like red bubble gum cutting across and down his chest and stomach. He always waved at us when we passed by on our bikes, but didn't ever say much. Maybe it just hurt him too much to talk. So we waved back, and out of respect, we never said hello either. Scar or no scar, he hadn't quit smoking.

And today, he was sure he had it all figured out: "I heard on the TV the other day on one of them news shows—not about this case, understand, but about something else—that there's a group of Satan worshippers who stole, first it was small animals like chickens, then animals big as cows, and eventually children, and tore them to bits. Worship, they called it. The newslady called it blood sacrifice and sacrilegious."

"You think that's what happened to the De Los Santos boy?" asked Junior the Clerk.

"Yes, sir, I do," answered smoking Old Man Charlie. "The blood of an innocent child would satisfy the devil more than a cow's or a chicken's, don't you think?"

"I guess so. But it all sounds too freaky, you know. I haven't heard of no Satan worshippers around here."

Old Man Charlie dragged on his cigarette a good long time and said to Junior the Clerk, "You think they'd make themselves obvious? 'Look at me, I kill for Satan. I love the devil.' They ain't going to knock on your door like the Jehovah's Witnesses and try to convert you like that, a big old 666 tattooed across their foreheads."

"I don't know which of them two groups visiting'd be worse, though," answered Junior the Clerk, scratching at his head.

The two men laughed, stopped, and crossed themselves.

I finished my drink and left.

That night I said my prayers like I'd never said them before. I dreamed of cows, and kittens, and they were being cut open, all of them screaming: meow-meow, moo-moo. I woke up sweating. I wanted to scream but knew I'd wake up my parents. They wouldn't let me out of the house if I did.

## XI

The first weeks after they found Danny were sort of a blur. No news of Danny's killer, and day in and out, parents checking up on us, then loosing their holds on us bit by bit as the days passed.

We spent as much time as possible at the ditch,

avoiding the Danny issue. Secretly, I thought we were all shaken, thrown off by it. We still had to figure it out for ourselves, especially after there was a report on the news about a guy who was arrested an hour away from us for molesting teen boys. That night I had the same dream about cows and kittens.

One day Mando said, "You think the same could've happened to Danny? A guy just trying to get off, and Danny fighting, but not being strong enough, or maybe like Mr. Charlie says—"

"Shut up about it!" said David. "What's the use trying to figure it out? Talk. That's all we do. Talk, talk, and more talk. What good is that!"

"Well, what can we do about it?" asked Mando. "What do we do?"

"Who do you think we are? Cops? Even they can't figure it out," answered David. "What I mean is, let's just let the guy rest. I read somewhere that in some cultures the more people talk about the dead the longer their souls are kept from going to heaven; they're like prisoners in space. What if it's true? And here you are, responsible for keeping a soul from moving on."

I noticed he wasn't using Danny's name. Maybe he actually believed what he was saying. Maybe he was just as scared as I was and was trying not to think about it at all. Out of sight, out of mind, no more fear, right?

"Juan, you were going to tell us about a dream you had?" said David.

"Ah, it's stupid. Just some silly stuff."

Pete said, "Tell us anyway."

"Nah, I can't even remember it anymore," I said. I didn't feel like being put in my place by David and his philosophizing on souls being imprisoned by dreams. Danny! Danny! Danny!

## XII

And so the summer passed.

Right before entering high school, we all began shopping for our new clothes, paper, pens, and other school materials, except for Pete, who went to visit family in a neighboring town across the border in Mexico. Not two days after coming back from visiting his grandfather, he went missing too. Everybody was very nervous again. My parents told me, "No two ways about it—you're staying in the house."

One day my mom sent me to the Korner Store for milk. "And come straight back home," she said. All the way to the store, and for the past few days, I'd been praying hard that Pete was just off somewhere stretching, straightening out whatever wasn't straight in his head. "Let him come back safe, God," I said over and over.

Old Man Charlie had come out to the store again. Still smoking and quoting from a newspaper article about the devil's churches all around the world.

"I don't want to say nothing," he told Junior the

Clerk, "because the boy is one of ours, but we have to expect the worst."

"I guess," agreed Junior the Clerk. "That way, if—*when* we find him, and he's doing well, we will be so happy to see him." He cut a case of beans and franks with a utility blade. "You really think he's been kidnapped by one of those devil-worshipping groups?"

"Hard to tell. With the De Los Santos boy found the way he was . . . You know, the police haven't yet found a clue about that one. Sometimes I ask myself where those boys go to school to become officers of the law."

"Oh, the white TV reporter, the pretty one, what's her name? Sue, I think it is. She was here yesterday," said Junior the Clerk.

"In the store?"

"No, just in the neighborhood. Poking around, asking questions. Everyone tight-lipped, not wanting to bring the bad salt on themselves. You know."

"Yeah." The old man breathed in the smoke of the cigarette, his eyes closed and taking in more air through his nose and then exhaling slowly.

Two days later, Pete showed up. He said he had run away. "For no reason," he told his parents, "sorry to worry you." They hugged him tight and let it slide about his running away and how much they were a wreck thinking they'd lost him. "We're just so happy you're back and not hurt." Everyone in his family hugged him. It was a big ball of arms, and crying for joy. The neighborhood breathed again.

To us, Pete said, "I'm just so embarrassed about my grandfather. I needed to figure things out for myself, so I took off."

His grandfather, he told us, "just got out of prison; he's eighty-five years old now. According to the viejitas on the street corners in Miguel Aleman, where my grandfather lives, he killed his own brother, who was six years younger than him. He did it about twenty years ago and was serving time ever since. I'd heard the story before.

"But last week, he took me to a cantina. He said, 'Here, drink this.' He put a glass of tequila in front of me. I didn't know what to do. He said, 'Drink it in one swallow, unless you're a mujeringa. It'll make a man of you.' I just looked at the tequila, holding it in my fingers. It looked just like water, but the smell alone was making me want to puke. '¡Tomatela!' he screamed, and slapped me on the back of the head, making me spill it on the bar. 'You make me sick!' me grito. I got up and left. '¡Mujeringa!' he screamed, then said to everyone there, 'There goes my nietesita, my little granddaughter. Her name is Petra.' I hate him!" He wiped his face.

A guy shouldn't have to hate his own grandfather like that, I thought.

"I got back from Miguel Aleman, and my father is all like, 'Mi'jo, so how did it go with your abuelo? He's a good man, made a mistake or two in his life. But he's paid for them. You know, mi'jo, you need to be more like him.' A drunk and a murderer is what he is. I'll never be like him. I hate him!"

But to me, all that mattered was that my friend was back. Losing Danny was hard and Danny was nothing to me but a guy at school. I couldn't even begin to think about losing one of my best friends. I wanted to hug Pete, like his family had done.

David got up from his place at the ditch. He walked up to Pete, shaking his head. I could have swore David was going to cry and hug him. Instead, he jumped on top of Pete and started punching him on the arms and chest and face. "You bastard!" he kept screaming. "I thought you were dead, you stupid idiot!" Mando and I had to pull him off.

David was breathing heavy, and Pete was bleeding from his nose.

"What's the matter with you?" I said. "He's back, and safe. It's something to be happy about."

David sat there, staring across the fields.

Pete crawled over to him and said, "I'm sorry, David."

"Don't you ever—"

"No, no, I won't."

"Because if it happened to you what happened to—to—"

Pete wrapped his arm around David. "It won't."

"You're my family. I can't lose you, too." IIe was crying.

We all were, and it must have looked like something

else, four guys crying in a ditch, all hugging on each other.

"You guys are my brothers. I don't know what I'd do if the same—" he said. Then he said, "Danny." He looked at us: "You're my brothers."

We hugged him tight. I heard him whispering, "Danny."

"Danny" just under his breath.

## XIII

Then it was the end of our summer. High school would be starting in a couple days.

I couldn't help thinking that David's crying after beating up Pete sounded like his mother calling out to him that summer night. He shook and shivered in Pete's arms, but when a guy goes through what we went through that summer, he either becomes a man earlier than expected, or he keeps it all inside. Then it explodes and there's nothing he can do about it. Then he's forced to talk about it.

But we had to learn to deal with what happened, each of us in our own way. We hadn't really talked about Danny, and maybe we didn't have to, maybe we never would. But David cried, and so did the rest of us, and he whispered Danny's name. That was enough for me.

David, Mando, Pete, and I learned something big that summer. I couldn't put it into words then, but I also knew I would not be able to keep quiet when I was ready. I wouldn't whisper anything. I'd have to shout.

On the first day of school, the English teacher said, "Take out a paper and write what you did this summer." Most of the students whined about it, but I pulled out my journal, already half-filled. I noticed I hadn't written anything in it since the last days of my eighth-grade year. So I left a blank page after the last entry. Then I began to write about that summer and what we saw and felt, and later when my teacher said, "Juan, this is some solid work," I said. "Yeah, thanks."

It was writing. It wasn't whispering.

# About the Author

The first book by René Saldaña, Jr., *The Jumping Tree,* was chosen by *Booklist* as one of its Top Ten Youth First Novels. Several of his poems and stories have appeared in literary journals.

René Saldaña, Jr., was born in McAllen, Texas, and grew up in nearby Peñitas, Texas. He graduated from Bob Jones University (B.A.), Clemson University (M.A.), and Georgia State University (Ph.D.) with degrees in English and creative writing. He has taught middle and high school. He and his wife, Tina, live in south Texas, where he teaches English and writing at the university level.